Joshua Wiggins and the Tough Challenge

*More stories about Joshua and his friends
for family devotions*

CHARLES BEAMER

BETHANY HOUSE PUBLISHERS

MINNEAPOLIS, MINNESOTA 55438

A Division of Bethany Fellowship, Inc.

Copyright © 1983
Charles Beamer
All Rights Reserved

Published by Bethany House Publishers
A Division of Bethany Fellowship, Inc.,
6820 Auto Club Road, Minneapolis, Minnesota 55438

Printed in the United States of America

Library of Congress Cataloging in Publication Data

Beamer, Charles.
  Joshua Wiggins & the tough challenge.

  Sequel to: Joshua Wiggins and the King's Kids.
  Summary: Joshua and his friends explore further ways of relating their Christian beliefs to events and feelings in their daily lives. A pertinent Bible verse and discussion questions follow each episode.
    1. Children—Prayer books and devotions—English.
2. Children—Religious life. [1. Christian life]
I. Title. II. Title: Joshua Wiggins and the tough challenge.

BV4870.B37   1982   248.8'2   82-25281
ISBN 0-87123-266-9

About the Author

CHARLES BEAMER is a free-lance writer and professional photographer. He has written several books and many articles. Mr. Beamer took his B.A. degree in English and History from North Texas State University and a Master's Degree in English from the University of Texas. He is married and the father of five children, ranging in age from 8 to 16. He is presently living in Denton, Texas. His first book in this series is *Joshua Wiggins and the King's Kids*.

Contents

Introduction

Jesus Christ was not, as some people have said, a wise Jewish carpenter; nor was He a famous Eastern philosopher. He was God, the Son of God, and He is the living Christ—Savior. Because He is what He is, He is Lord—Master of those who acknowledge Him for what He is. As Lord He demands full and wholehearted obedience—not to a call of power or a call of knowledge or a call of worldly wisdom, but to a love call.

WEEK ONE

"Am I Saved?"

Day 1

Sunday Morning

While the church service offering was being taken, Joshua Wiggins smiled at Chris Dobbs, who was sitting beside him. Joshua glanced at the other King's Kids along the same row: Lori Matthews, Janie Warren, and Denise Kibler. Beyond them were Sammy Fletcher and Richard Wolfe, who was writing a note on the back of a program. Joshua turned and looked toward the back of the sanctuary.

In the shadows under the balcony were some of the younger brothers and sisters of the King's Kids. It occurred to Joshua that most of them were not followers of the King. Seth Jensen, Dotty's younger brother, was one of those. He was sitting beside David Matthews, Lori's little brother. David had become a follower of Jesus, the King, when he was five, Joshua remembered. Near those two boys sat Randy Dobbs, Chris' younger brother; Randy was hunched down as if he were trying not to be seen. And behind him, way in the back near the doors, sat a dim figure Joshua could barely recognize. *Frank Rothman finally came!* Joshua thought, then quickly asked himself, *I wonder what changed his mind?*

In a few minutes, Pastor Burton began his sermon. Joshua turned toward the front to listen. Out of the corner of his eye, he saw Richard put down his note, and he heard Lori and Janie stop whispering to each other.

"The message I am to bring you today," Pastor Burton began, "is a challenge. It is a challenge that has no 'ifs' about it. Jesus himself issued the challenge, and James later repeated it in these words: 'So get rid of all that is wrong in your life, both inside and outside, and humbly be glad for the wonderful message we have received, for it is able to save our souls as it takes hold of our hearts. And remember, it is a message to obey, not just to listen to.' "* Pastor Burton walked around the lectern and looked at individuals in the congregation.

"We all love Jesus," he resumed. "We all know He is a loving, kind, merciful and forgiving person. But do we also know that all authority has been given to Him? In fact, He has given us His authority so that we can be like Him, so that we can be holy and pure, so that we can love. In other words, Jesus gives us all the power we need to obey all His commands. Someday, He himself will ask us, 'Did you obey me—or not? Did you do what I said to do—or did you merely think what I said was nice, comforting, but impossible?' "

As Pastor Burton continued looking at members of the congregation, Joshua felt a thrill inside himself. He glanced at Chris and saw that Chris, too, was sitting up straighter.

"The secret to obeying Christ is love; and Christian love is different from worldly love," Pastor Burton was saying. "Worldly love is a feeling, a desire; when the thing desired goes away or becomes worn out, so does worldly love. But Christian love—the love of Christ for us and our love for one another—will never, never go away or become worn out! With Christ's love in us, we will always be able to love and to obey."

When the service was over, Joshua and Chris left the sanctuary together, still feeling the specialness of Christ's love for them. As if sharing a very special secret, they smiled at each other.

Ahead of them walked Seth Jensen and David Matthews, and Seth looked angry. Abruptly he turned and shoved David. "What makes you think you're so special!" he snapped at David. Seth then gave the older boys and David a glowering, sullen look and ran off toward the neighborhood where they all lived near one another.

"What was that all about?" Chris asked David, glancing at the adults who were streaming around them, staring.

David, his expression filled with confusion and embarrassment, said nothing. He shrugged, lowered his head, and hurried away from the church.

". . . it isn't enough just to have faith. You must also do good to prove that you have it. Faith that doesn't show itself by good works is no faith at all—it is dead and useless" (James 2:17).

_____
*James 1:21-22a

10

Discussion Questions:
1. Is Seth Jensen saved? When was David saved?
2. How can you tell whether or not a person is saved? How do you know whether or not you yourself are truly saved?
3. Why is it important that Christ's commands be obeyed and not merely listened to?

Day 2

Sunday Afternoon

Chris brushed his shiny black hair away from his face and looked at Joshua with bright, black eyes. "Do you think we ought to go after Seth?"

Joshua, who was shorter and stockier than Chris and had thick, brown-blond hair, looked back toward the church doors. He caught sight of Lori Matthews coming out with Denise and Janie. "Lori!" he called, going toward her through the outgoing crowd. She held her long, light brown hair away from her blue eyes as a breeze gusted past. "Lori," Josh said quietly, "do you know what's wrong between David and Seth?"

Lori laughed; she looked at Janie, who was smiling at Chris. Lori motioned to Josh, and they started walking toward their neighborhood together, followed by Chris, Janie, and Denise, whose pale blond hair streamed past her tall, thin body. "David and Seth are friends," Lori began, "but they fight a lot. It goes back to when Seth's sister, Dotty, was mad at Janie over Richard. Dotty started all that gossip about Janie, and when I stuck up for Janie, Dotty got mad at me, too. Since then, she's gotten this—this *thing* about us King's Kids. She says we're a bunch of snobs, and she's tried to convince Seth that he ought to stay away from us—including my brother, David." She paused to look up and down the busy street before they crossed it and entered their neighborhood. "I'm afraid David hasn't helped the problem much."

"How come?" Joshua asked, catching sight of David walking by himself a block ahead of them.

Lori looked toward her brother. "Well, he's been a Christian since he was five, but lately, since we King's Kids have started getting serious about what we believe, he's become uncomfortable."

"Like he isn't really sure about what he believes?" Josh asked.

"No—about whether or not he's really saved."

"Have you talked with him?"

12

"I've tried—and so has Dad. But David is shy; he gets embarrassed easily and won't talk, except to Seth. And the times I've heard him talking to Seth—when he didn't know I was listening—he's come on very strongly, even saying Seth was going to hell."

Josh frowned. "Maybe Chris and I should talk to David, try to get him into the King's Kids."

"He thinks the club is just for us older kids, that we'd treat him like a baby."

"You mean 'cause we're in junior high and he's in elementary school?"

Lori nodded. "That keeps a lot of kids away from us—kids like Randy Dobbs and Seth Jensen."

Josh said, "We should tell him that people of any age—including Janie's grandfather, Pa-pa Warren—can be King's Kids." Josh grinned, looking ahead again at the younger boy trudging along. "After all, how old you are—or who you are—isn't what matters."

"If you want to know what God wants you to do, ask him, and he will gladly tell you, for he is always ready to give a bountiful supply of wisdom to all who ask him; he will not resent it. But when you ask him, be sure that you really expect him to tell you, for a doubtful mind will be as unsettled as a wave of the sea that is driven and tossed by the wind; and every decision you then make will be uncertain, as you turn first this way, and then that. If you don't ask with faith, don't expect the Lord to give you any solid answer" (James 1:5-8).

Discussion Questions:
1. What would you guess Seth Jensen's problems are? In what way is he like a wave driven and tossed by the wind? What would you guess David Matthews' problem is? In what way is he like a wave?
2. If we are truly and totally to obey Christ's commands, we must not allow doubts to control our thoughts. But Satan loves to put doubts in our minds, and does it often. What, therefore, should we do when we have doubts?
3. If we are to obey Christ, how are we to know what He wants us to do? For example, what are some ways Joshua could find out what Christ would want him to do about David Matthews? How could David learn what he is supposed to do?

Day 3

Sunday Night

That night, after the evening worship service, Joshua led the King's Kids to the church's youth director, Steve. Josh asked him to pray with them for guidance about how to help David, Seth, Randy, and Frank Rothman.

"You see," Joshua said, "what we want to do is talk to them—tell them what we think they should do and explain what the King's Kids are doing." He glanced at Chris and the others and grinned sheepishly. "But because that's what *we* want to do, we thought we should pray and find out what *God* wants us to do."

They went to a Sunday school classroom, sat in a circle, and held hands. In the quiet of the room, it took some time before their own thoughts began to quiet. Then Steve began softly, "Lord, we ask that you give us the wisdom you promise. Intrude upon our own wishes and show us how to help these we're concerned about: Seth, David, Randy, Frank, and any others to whom you would lead us." He stopped, and they all sat in silence.

Joshua remembered a time when he would have become uncomfortable in the silence, thinking about all the things he could be doing. But now, he was surprised to find how good the peacefulness of the room felt. He was glad to be with friends, waiting for God to speak to their hearts.

A rustling of pages disturbed the silence. Steve began to read: " 'I have loved you even as the Father has loved me. Live within my love. When you obey me you are living in my love, just as I obey my Father and live in his love. I have told you this so that you will be filled with my joy. Yes, your cup of joy will overflow! I demand that you love each other as much as I love you.' "*

When Joshua felt Chris squeeze his left hand, he squeezed Lori's

---

*John 15:9-12

14

hand on his right. He opened his eyes and looked around. The youth director asked, "Is there anything that can't be conquered with the love of Christ?"

"But what are we supposed to *do*?" Denise asked impatiently. "*How* are we supposed to show David and the others Christ's love?"

"Let's get him together with my grandfather," Janie Warren suggested. "I don't know anybody better at showing Christ's love than Pa-pa is."

"What about the others we were praying for?" Denise asked, still not convinced. "Shouldn't we talk to them? I mean, are we just supposed to sit back and do nothing?"

"Is finding ways to love someone the way Christ loves us doing 'nothing'?" Steve asked. "In fact, did you know that our showing Christ's love is the main way God is made visible to others?"

Denise slowly smiled, looking at Janie. "Yes," she said, "I know."

"Then keep on praying—that God will give us opportunities to show His love to those we've been praying about. And if you don't doubt that He will make those opportunities, He will make them!"

" 'I have loved you even as the Father has loved me. Live within my love' " (John 15:9).

Discussion Questions:
1. What did Denise want to do about the problems with which the King's Kids were dealing? Tell about at least one time you were tempted to do the same kind of thing. What happened?
2. In what ways can we show other people the love Jesus Christ has for us? How does loving other people "make God visible"? How can obeying Jesus and living in His love fill us with joy?
3. Was Christ's love something He *felt*, or was it something He *did*, regardless of who the person was? How can we answer Christ's call to love when it means loving someone we don't like, someone who's hurt us, or someone who is very different from the way we are?

15

Day 4

David

David Matthews reluctantly went with his sister, Lori, to spend Monday evening with Janie Warren. Almost without his realizing it, the girls managed to leave him alone with Pa-pa Warren in the den.

David sat on the edge of the sofa, fidgeting and feeling uncomfortable. He occasionally glanced at Pa-pa, while wondering how to leave without hurting the old man's feelings. He wished he hadn't agreed to come with Lori; but, still, there was something about the way the old man was looking at him that made him feel he was supposed to be there.

"Why're you staring at me?" David finally asked impatiently.

Pa-pa's wrinkled, squarish face took on a determined look; he leaned forward and said, "Your friends are worried about you."

David quickly scooted against the back of the sofa and folded his arms. "I don't have any friends."

"Your best friend is Jesus Christ; and you've got other friends *He* has sent to be near you, to pray for you, and to care about you."

David sat upright. "Pray for me?"

"Yes; to pray that you won't think you're alone in your battle with Satan," Pa-pa said gently, moving to the sofa to sit near David. "He's using one of his most powerful weapons—doubt."

"Your friend, Grandpa Wiggins, once told me that I had the armor of God," David mumbled, then suddenly looked at Pa-pa. "But Grandpa Wiggins died—and I don't feel the armor anymore!"

"Thank the Lord Dan Wiggins is in heaven," Pa-pa said firmly, giving David a piercing look. Then he gave a slight grin. "And I'll bet he's cheering you on right now!"

David's shoulders slumped and his eyes became tearful. "Do you think I'll ever be there—in heaven?"

"That's between you and God. But have you given yourself—*all* of

16

yourself—to the Lord? If you haven't, then the armor won't do you any good because you don't really believe it will."

"It's—hard . . . ," David said haltingly, glancing at Pa-pa. "It's hard to believe things like the armor—and even God—are for real."

"They won't ever seem real if you don't turn yourself over to God in faith. If you just dabble your toes in believing, you won't ever experience the *real*-ness of Christ. And if you keep your eyes down, you won't ever see the friends you really do have, the friends who are trying to show Christ's love for you by what they do."

"But am I going to heaven?"

Pa-pa laid one hand on David's left shoulder. "Is Jesus Christ really your master? Do you do what He says?"

"Sometimes."

"When you feel like it?"

"Y—yes," David admitted.

"And do you think you have to act good before Christ will love you?"

"Sort of," David said, squirming.

Pa-pa's hand tightened firmly on David's shoulder. "Then you're trying to be a Christian on your own power, rather than Christ's. It's by *His* power that we do the things that prove we're saved—like loving others even when they hurt or hate us."

David gave Pa-pa a peculiar look. "Is that why Seth Jensen won't listen to me—'cause he sees that I don't really love him?"

Pa-pa leaned back, smiling. "Do you play around creeks?"

David looked at him and blinked, puzzled. "Sure, when I can."

"Ever fall in one?"

Embarrassed, David nodded.

"Anybody see you—and laugh?"

David tried to stifle a grin. "They sure did."

"Maybe Seth Jensen feels you're laughing at him about something."

David looked at the sofa cushions, frowning. After a moment, he said, "Maybe he doesn't like for me to say he's going to hell and I'm not." He looked questioningly at Pa-pa Warren.

Gently, the old man said, "It wouldn't be good if you were being hard on Seth about something you are afraid will happen to you yourself."

David's expression twisted in pain and tears brimmed his eyelids.

"Do you, David Matthews, believe in your heart that Jesus Christ is the crucified and risen Savior and that He should be Lord of your life? 'For if you tell others with your own mouth that Jesus Christ is your Lord, and believe in your own heart that God has raised him from the dead, you will be saved.' "*

Tears slowly ran down David's cheeks as he nodded.

"Are you ready to give yourself to Him—completely?"

"Yes."

Pa-pa closed his eyes. "Say this with me," the old man gently urged. David repeated the words as Pa-pa spoke them: "Lord Jesus, I've sinned and hurt you. I need you. Thank you for being God's Son, for dying on the cross for my sins. I open my heart to you—and I give you my life as my Savior and Lord. Take control of me. Amen."

In a while, Pa-pa asked, "What day is today?"

Looking surprised, David raised his head as he wiped his cheeks. He told Pa-pa the day and date.

"Okay," Pa-pa Warren said firmly. "I want you to go home and write down what you just prayed. Put the date on it, sign it, and put the piece of paper in a safe place. The next time Satan makes you worried that you aren't saved, I want you to take out the paper and show it to him. Don't let Satan make you think he, or anything else, can take away from you what God himself has given!"

David sighed. "And that's what I'm suppose to tell Seth, too, isn't it? I mean, about how Christ died and rose for us."

"Yes," Pa-pa stated, "and don't forget your friends."

"I won't forget them—or you," David promised as he stood to leave.

"If you believe that Jesus is the Christ—that he is God's Son and your Savior—then you are a child of God. And all who love the Father love his children too. So you can find out how much you love God's children—your brothers and sisters in the Lord—by how much you love and obey God. Loving God means doing what he tells us to do, and really, that isn't hard at all; for every child of God can obey him, defeating sin and evil pleasure by trusting Christ to help him" (1 John 5:1-4).

Discussion Questions:
1. If you, like David Matthews, have doubts about your salvation, will you pray right now the prayer Pa-pa Warren had David pray and do what Pa-pa said David should do with the prayer?
2. If you still have doubts, or if you have not experienced the joy of salvation or have not succeeded at defeating sin, what is the cause

---

*Romans 10:9

of that problem? How does the Scripture on page 18 say we are to defeat Satan, sin, and evil pleasure? Can we do so with our own power? What will happen if we try to use our own power to defeat Satan?

3. What are some things that might happen to David Matthews next? What does the Word say he should do next? (See, for example, Acts 2:44-45.)

Seth Takes the Plunge

"And I guess I was so busy trying to feel like I was saved," David was telling Seth, "that I—I had to make you feel like you were worse than me. I'm sorry. Will you forgive me for acting like a snob?"

"Sure," Seth said uncomfortably. "I guess so." He continued staring at the prayer David had written and signed. He looked at David. "I did feel I was worse than you were. In fact, I felt—feel like nothing, like I'm worthless. My parents, my sister, my teacher, everybody is always down on me, telling me what I do is wrong, stupid." He slumped as if he were about to cry, but stopped himself.

David stepped closer to him. "Then you need to know Jesus. That's what Pa-pa Warren helped me understand: that I need to let Christ take over."

"Take over *what*?" Seth asked, frowning uncertainly.

"*Everything*," David said firmly. "Your feelings of being nothing, your fears—like I was having—and everything else."

Seth's frown deepened. "I'd feel funny, you know—asking someone I can't see to—to come into my heart and make me different."

"It might seem like a tough thing to do, but once we've given Jesus control, we have the power to be good. By ourselves, of course, we're bad. Most people don't think so, but we are. Some people act good 'cause they're afraid of the police and what people might think of them if they did wrong. But you know other people—like Pastor Burton and Pa-pa Warren—who act good because the Spirit of Jesus is living inside them. And because they obey what His Spirit says, you and I can see what Jesus is like, what He can do."

"I guess so," Seth said. He glanced at David. "But what about the other people in church who claim to be Christians, but who—well, who don't act like what you told me Jesus is like?"

"Don't worry about them," David said. "My father says they're God's problem. All we've got to worry about is letting Jesus have *us*."

Seth suddenly laughed and relaxed. Almost shyly he looked at David. "You've sure changed."

"It was praying this prayer—and meaning it," David said, pointing to the piece of paper Seth was holding. "No matter what your sister says, you and me are a lot alike. Both of us need Jesus so we won't be afraid, so we can have help in doing what's right. If we don't get His help, we'll go on feeling stupid, fighting with everybody, and messing up."

"You mean, if I pray this prayer with you I won't be afraid again, I won't mess up again?" Seth asked hopefully.

"My father says that depends on how much we obey Christ. If we learn what He said and *do* it, then we'll be safe, even if Satan makes bad things happen to us."

Seth took a deep breath, rubbing one edge of the piece of paper. "Okay," he said, grinning nervously. "I think I was ready before, but—but I kept getting mad at you. Now I'm sure I'm ready." He took another deep breath, closed his eyes, and prayed the prayer.

"[The men of Israel] said to [Peter] and to the other apostles, 'Brothers, what should we do?' And Peter replied, 'Each one of you must turn from sin, return to God, and be baptized in the name of Jesus Christ for the forgiveness of your sins; then you also shall receive this gift, the Holy Spirit. For Christ promised him to each one of you who has been called by the Lord our God, and to our children and even to those in distant lands!' " (Acts 2:37b-39).

Discussion Questions:
1. What do you suppose led Seth to salvation, even more forcefully than David's efforts? What, according to the Scripture above, should Seth do next? What promise can he expect to receive from Christ? How do you think David Matthews has demonstrated that Christ's promise is for real?
2. Why do you suppose that many Christians never experience the joy Christ promised in John 15:11 (quoted in the Day 3 chapter) or the gift of the Holy Spirit?
3. Is Seth "home free"? In other words, is his battle over? What do you think might happen to him next?

WEEK TWO

"I Don't Feel Anything"

Day 1

Down, Down, Down

As Seth Jensen was going out the front door of his home, his mother called out, "Seth, before you go anywhere, I want you to rake the leaves in the back yard!"

Seth paused, his hand on the doorknob. "I'll do it tomorrow," he called back.

"That's what you said yesterday," his mother said, coming into the hallway with an annoyed look on her face. "If we're going to keep giving you an allowance, you'll have to do the few things we ask you to do."

Seth's expression wrinkled. "I don't feel like it, Mom!" he said, twisting the knob.

"You feel like going out, don't you? Where are you going anyway? To the clubhouse?"

Seth nodded.

"Well, if you feel like playing, you can work up the energy to rake the yard." Her expression stiffened. "And by the way, have you done your homework?"

Seth hung his head, hiding his pale blue eyes; a strand of white-blond hair fell across his forehead.

His mother pointed a finger at him. "You do your homework now, and when you finish it, rake the yard. Then you may go to the clubhouse."

"Aw, Mom!" Seth protested, looking angrily at her.

"Now!" she insisted.

"But the King's Kids are waiting. I told David and Joshua—"

"Just because you've joined that club doesn't mean you can stop doing what your father and I ask you to do. We were hoping that once you became friends with Joshua and his club you'd start obeying us better. But it doesn't seem that joining the club has made one bit of difference."

Seth gave her a sullen look. He dragged his feet as he went up the hall and toward his room, muttering, "*Nothing* makes any difference!"

"Then Jesus said to the disciples, 'If anyone wants to be a follower of mine, let him deny himself and take up his cross and follow me. For anyone who keeps his life for himself shall lose it; and anyone who loses his life for me shall find it again' " (Matt. 16:24-25).

Discussion Questions:
1. Seth has prayed the "sinner's prayer" with David, and he might say that he is saved. But is he a follower of Jesus? How do you know?
2. What connection is there between our obedience to our parents and our obedience to Jesus Christ? (See Ephesians 6:1-3.)
3. What do you think David or Joshua might say to Seth now?

24

DAY 2

Escape

Seth made his escape as soon as he finished doing some of his homework. As he left the house, he yelled, "I'll rake the yard—tomorrow." He slammed the door and set off toward the field. Beyond it was the woods, and in the woods was the King's Kids' clubhouse.

While he was running across the field, he noticed a boy about his own age standing in the shadows at the edge of the woods. Seth shrugged, figuring some new kid was trying to spy on the clubhouse.

When Seth climbed the steps up the tree trunk and went into the first-story room of the clubhouse, he saw no one. Immediately, anger rushed into him, and he felt like crying. *I told her!* he thought. *I told her they were waiting for me—and now they've gone. Why does she ALWAYS have to be against me!*

"Seth?" called a voice from one of the upstairs rooms. "Is that you?" A trap door opened above his head, and David's face appeared. "Why're you lookin' so sad? Come on up."

Seth followed David up two more stories. As he entered the top room another voice startled him.

"What happened to you?" Joshua Wiggins asked gently.

Seth shrugged as he turned. "My mother is always trying to keep me from doing what I want to do."

Josh looked at David, then back to Seth. "Did you have a fight with her?" he asked.

Seth shrugged again and wiped a strand of pale hair off his forehead. "We fight almost every day."

"Even after you prayed to be saved?"

Seth looked blankly at Joshua, and he felt a strange kind of anger creep into his mind. He lowered his gaze. "That prayer doesn't seem to have made any difference." He looked at Josh, then at David. "In fact, I don't feel anything at all."

"What did you expect to feel?"

Seth closed the trap door and sat on the floor, arms folded. "I don't know. Happy, I guess. Or at least not stupid and wrong."

"But nothing has changed?"

"No!" Seth said, letting a bit of his anger slip through. "Well—if anything, I feel more down than ever. Worthless."

"Have you been reading the Bible David gave you?"

Seth shook his head.

"Have you been praying?"

"No."

"Are you still going to the front in church next Sunday to say that Jesus is your Lord—your master?"

"I guess so." Seth squirmed, tightly crossing his legs.

Josh sat beside him. "Are you doing what Jesus tells you to do?"

Seth again looked blankly at him. "What d'you mean?"

"Are you obeying your new master—or are you still listening to your old one?"

Seth's anger rose as he stood, his hands held stiffly at his sides. "What 'old master'?"

"Satan," Joshua said. "Who do you think is trying to keep you down, angry, disobedient?"

"No one is," Seth stammered. "I mean, I just—I'm *trying* to be good."

"*Trying* is a lot different from giving up your life to Jesus."

"Giving up?" Seth asked stiffly, then sighed and let his shoulders slump. "Is that why I don't feel any different—'cause I'm letting Satan make me do things on my own?"

Josh nodded. "Satan doesn't want you to change—to repent. He'll keep on encouraging you to be your old self—angry and proud and frustrated—until you forget about trying to be a follower of Jesus. Your only other choice is to give up to Christ and let *His* power protect you from Satan."

Seth laughed nervously. "You sound like my mother, making me do my homework."

"Grandpa Wiggins used to say that God gives each of us freedom to obey *someone*—either Satan, who wants us to think we're doing the best we can do, or Christ—and our parents."

Seth nodded slowly, then lowered himself through the trap door and started to go down the ladder. He paused and said, "By the way, I saw a strange kid hanging around the edge of the woods."

Joshua nodded and waited for Seth to leave. He and David watched him go slowly back through the woods and disappear. Then

Joshua looked at David. "We've gotta pray for him," he said.

> *"Create in me a new, clean heart, O God, filled with clean thoughts and right desires . . . . Restore to me again the joy of your salvation, and make me willing to obey you . . . . It is a broken spirit you want—remorse and penitence. A broken and a contrite heart, O God, you will not ignore"* (Psalm 51:10, 12, 17).

Discussion Questions:
1. Why was Seth having doubts and problems about his salvation, even after he prayed to be saved?
2. How can feeling badly about ourselves—having a broken spirit— lead us closer to God?
3. If you were with Joshua and David, how would you pray for Seth?

Day 3

Dotty's Advice

Seth knocked softly on the door of his sister's room. When she said, "Come in," he went inside and glumly sat on her bed. She was lying down watching her TV.

"What's wrong with you?" Dotty asked, keeping her eyes on the TV screen.

Seth shrugged. "Everybody's down on me. Mom's always making me do things, Dad's been giving me hateful looks, and those friends of mine—or those guys I *thought* were my friends. . . ."

Dotty sat up against her headboard; her expression was a mixture of grin and frown. "I told you not to hang around David and Josh and those other kids. Janie Warren is the worst of them; she thinks she's a solid gold angel. And the rest of those 'King's Turkeys,' or whatever they call themselves, think they're better than everybody else."

"Yeah," Seth said uncertainly; he wanted understanding, a friend, but on the other hand he didn't quite agree with his sister's opinion.

Dotty snorted and folded her arms. Her gaze wandered back to the TV set. "It's their *attitude* that bothers me," she muttered, folding her arms more tightly. "They go around junior high smiling and speaking to one another like they have something special that none of the rest of us can have."

Seth sat up straighter. He glanced at the couple yelling and fighting on the TV program, and for some reason, he felt even more uncomfortable about Dotty's opinion. Cautiously, not wanting to make her mad after he had sought her out, he said, "Well, they're not really hiding—"

Dotty silenced him with a bitter glare. "You came in here whining about your friends, and now you're sticking up for them. If they're so great, you just keep going with them to that church—which is one place I wouldn't set foot in again if my life depended on it! And in the meantime, stop bothering me."

28

Seth left her room and closed the door so she wouldn't yell at him to shut it. As he went into his own room, some words Pastor Burton had used suddenly popped into his mind. As he sat on his bed trying to do his homework the words came again: "Shallow soil . . . shallow soil. . . ."

" 'Now here is the explanation of the story I told about the farmer planting grain: The hard path where some of the seeds fell represents the heart of a person who hears the Good News about the Kingdom and doesn't understand it; then Satan comes and snatches away the seeds from his heart. The shallow, rocky soil represents the heart of a man who hears the message and receives it with real joy, but he doesn't have much depth in his life, and the seeds don't root very deeply, and after a while when trouble comes, or persecution begins because of his beliefs, his enthusiasm fades, and he drops out' " (Matt. 13:18-21).

Discussion Questions:
1. How would you describe Dotty Jensen? Toward what goal or purpose does she influence her brother?
2. Why do you suppose Seth remembered Pastor Burton's quotation from Matthew about "shallow soil"? In what way is God at work in Seth?
3. Silently answer this question: Are you a hard path (Matt. 13:19); shallow, rocky soil (Matt. 13:20-21); ground covered with thistles (Matt. 13:22); or good ground (Matt. 13:23)? Which kind of ground (growing place for the seeds of God's Word) do you suppose Jesus thinks you are?

Day 4

Which Side?

Seth was too troubled to do his homework. His mind was carrying on a conversation with itself, and the conversation was growing into an argument.

His mother came into his room about ten o'clock and told him to put on his pajamas and go to sleep. She kissed him good night and slipped from the room—without noticing that he was about to burst with the questions that were swimming around his mind.

Seth was soon in bed, but he could not go to sleep. As he lay in the darkness, the argument in his mind swirled faster and faster.

One voice cried, *Just do what you want to do! You don't have to listen to Josh or David—or anybody but yourself!*

A more quiet voice answered, *But David and Josh like me.*

They just want you to do what they say, sneered the first voice. *Like your mother and father, they're always trying to get you to do their dirty work.*

But I can't fight everyone on my own! the second voice protested. *I'm tired of fighting and being afraid and upset all the time. And I want to do what's right—what's good and clean and—fair. I don't like fighting and arguments!*

As the debate went on and on, Seth began to identify one voice—the one that wanted him to stay away from Josh and David and to do what *he* wanted to do—with his sister and her friends—and with Satan.

When he realized that the selfish voice was indeed a voice of darkness—Satan's voice—he became deeply frightened that it was *inside* him. But he also realized that the quiet voice was the voice of his own spirit, that part of himself that was the best—and most like the Jesus he had heard about. Suddenly, he wished he had read the Bible David had given him; he told himself that he would begin reading more—tomorrow.

30

For a while then, he relaxed, comfortable with the thought of what he planned to do. But then he thought, *What if I die tonight?* Quickly, the other voice argued, *Don't be silly! You won't die tonight—or tomorrow night. There's plenty of time to make a decision. Why rush into something just because some of your so-called friends want to use you?*

Seth twisted over in his bed, growing troubled again. He felt fear and a pulling in the pit of his stomach. The feeling rose up inside him powerfully, and he almost began to cry. As he fought back his tears, he rapidly thought, *I'm sick of fighting Mom and Dad and being angry! I want to be like Josh and David—smiling outside, clean inside.* The part of him that was holding back his tears added, *Why should you give up yourself, and everything you want to do and be, to Jesus?*

The answer was so strong, so firm and loving, that his arguments vanished. *Be clean! Be free! Be at peace!*

Seth sobbed and began to cry a flood of tears. From deep, deep inside himself, feelings flooded forth—feelings of guilt, memories of things he had said and done to hurt his parents, things he had done to hurt his friends, even things he had done to hurt himself and to make himself fail. The feeling in the pit of his stomach grew so strong that he felt as if it were emptying him, turning him inside out. Abruptly he got out of bed and knelt on the floor. Burying his face in the covers, he sobbed, "Please forgive me, Lord Jesus, for hurting you. Take me away from Satan and—make me your child."

He felt suddenly as if winter had become spring; he felt like dancing, singing. At the same time, however, he felt strangely quiet and shy in the newness. He felt afraid to do anything, to even say anything, lest the wonderful feeling should go away. So, after thinking a long while about Jesus and being inside the wonderful peacefulness he knew was inside and around him, Seth climbed back into bed. He pulled up the warm covers and quickly fell asleep.

"That evening the disciples were meeting behind locked doors, in fear of the Jewish leaders, when suddenly Jesus was standing there among them! After greeting them, he showed them his hands and side. And how wonderful was their joy as they saw their Lord! He spoke to them again and said, 'As the Father has sent me, even so I am sending you.' Then he breathed on them and told them, 'Receive the Holy Spirit'" (John 20:19-22).

Discussion Questions:
1. In what ways has Seth been changed?

2. What problem has Seth faced in the past that he is likely to face again—probably very soon? How can he now face that problem differently?
3. Seth may not want to brag or even talk about his change, but what will Jesus want him to do from now on?

Day 5

Mrs. Wards

The following day was Saturday, and after Seth ate breakfast, he could hardly sit still. He was excited—so excited that he couldn't decide what to do first. He finally concluded that if he really had turned his life over to Jesus, he should start by asking Him what to do that day. So, he went into his room and prayed.

Seth didn't quite know what to expect in the way of an answer. He waited—and waited. But nothing happened. Finally, about ten o'clock, he got tired of waiting and left the house. He was hoping to meet some of the King's Kids so he could be with them, but as he walked around the neighborhood he saw no one. No one, that is, except old Mrs. Wards—who, like all old people, always had made Seth uneasy.

She was walking down the long street between the neighborhood and the field. She was bent over, carrying a grocery sack that seemed almost empty. Seth wondered what she was doing, and why she didn't have her little dog with her. So, lacking anything else to do, he followed her.

Before long she stopped, looked from side to side, then stooped down and picked up a pop can. She thrust it into her sack and hurried on up the street as if she didn't want to be seen. He thought, *She must be ashamed of picking up aluminum cans on the street—wow! She must really need the money.* It did not occur to him that he was no longer uneasy looking at an old person, a person who once had represented death and sickness.

Seth had followed Mrs. Wards for three blocks when an old, faded green Chevy passed him and stopped at the intersection nearest the old lady. While the driver was waiting for traffic to pass so she could turn, she saw the old lady pick up a can. As Seth caught up with Mrs. Wards, he heard the driver laughing—louder and louder—at Mrs. Wards.

Angered, Seth ran ahead—as the car turned the corner and smoked its way toward a house with an unmown yard. When Seth caught up with Mrs. Wards, he saw that the old lady was crying.

"It's all right," he said gently, putting one hand on her back.

Surprised, she flinched and turned quickly to peer at him. But just as quickly, she looked away and began walking up the street.

Seth followed. "May I help you pick up cans?" he asked. "I can stomp them flat so you can put more into your sack."

Mrs. Wards said nothing and stared straight ahead. So, he crossed to the other side of the street, picked a can out of the weeds at the curbside, stomped it on the pavement, and carried it to Mrs. Wards. She didn't look at him even when he slipped the can into her sack.

They walked perhaps a mile in that manner. Mrs. Wards covered one side of the streets they followed, and Seth covered the other side. He flattened fifteen cans and put them into her sack, but she did not look at him even once. Finally, they returned to her home.

With her head lowered, she turned to go up her driveway. Seth waited in the street. Mrs. Wards stopped, turned slowly, and smiled at him. "Thank you," she said, loudly and with some hesitation.

"You're welcome," he said loudly, realizing she was hard of hearing.

"Oh, yes, I'll pay you for your share," she said quickly.

"No, no," Seth said more loudly still, walking toward her. "I said, you're welcome! I liked helping you!"

She took a step toward him. "You did?"

"Yes, ma'am," Seth said. "And I'd like to help you again. I'll keep people like that woman in the green car from laughing at you."

Mrs. Wards looked down at her sack as she folded the top of it. "I've seen her throw out some of the beer cans we've been picking up," she said quietly, then gave a smile. "So, I guess even if she laughs, she's helping me without knowing it."

"Well, you can count on me to help," Seth said firmly. "When do you want to go out again?"

Mrs. Wards wrinkled her face thoughtfully. "I still need eighteen dollars for my gas bill, so I guess I'll have to go out Monday."

"I'll meet you here at four o'clock," Seth said, figuring that would give him thirty minutes after school to rake the back yard.

"You're sure you don't mind?" Mrs. Wards asked hesitantly.

Seth reached out and squeezed her hand. "See you Monday!" he called as he ran off toward his home.

34

" 'Humble men are very fortunate!' [Jesus] told them, 'for the Kingdom of Heaven is given to them. Those who mourn are fortunate! for they shall be comforted. The meek and lowly are fortunate! for the whole wide world belongs to them' " (Matt. 5:3-5).

Discussion Questions:
1. Early Saturday, what was Seth's prayer? Was it answered?
2. In what way was Jesus Christ present with Mrs. Wards on Saturday?
3. In what ways has Seth changed?

WEEK THREE

"Be My Friend"

Day 1

Gifts

Seth Jensen and David Matthews were riding their ten-speed bikes to the shopping center when they saw a familiar figure walking slowly toward them. He was taller and older than they, and muscular from playing football. "Frank Rothman," David said.

When they were about to go past him, he looked at them and smiled. His curly black hair and black eyes complemented his deeply tanned skin and stylish clothes; but his eyes, David noticed, had a sad, lonely look. "Where're you guys goin'?" he asked the younger boys.

"To buy my mother a birthday card," David answered, pleased that Frank had stopped to talk with them. He, like most of the younger boys, was impressed by Frank—even if he had been dropped from the junior high football team.

"Mind if I go with you?" Frank asked as he turned around and began to jog along next to them.

"No," Seth replied, then asked quickly, "What'cha been doin'?"

Frank shrugged. "Oh, looking at new swimming suits," he said lightly—as if, Seth thought, he really didn't care what he'd been doing. Frank suddenly smiled at them again. "Say, why don't you two come swimming afterward at my house. My pool's a lot less crowded than the public one." He looked at each of them for an answer.

"Sure," David said, hardly able to believe that Frank would invite them. He stopped pedaling. "When?"

"As soon as you get through doing whatever it was you said you had to do," Frank said.

37

Seth and David agreed to go swimming later, and Frank followed them to the gift shop. When David had chosen a card for his mother and was about to pay for it, Frank took it from him. To the cashier he said, "Just put this on our charge account."

The clerk smiled and nodded, then wrote up the charge. "Thank you, Frank," she said as the boys were leaving.

"You didn't have to do that," David said as he clipped the card onto his bike's carrier rack. "I'd saved the money for the card and a gift."

"You're going to buy her a gift, too?" Frank asked. "You should've gotten one back there and let me put it on our tab." He started to go back to the store.

David gave a confused glance to Seth. He felt reluctant to tell Frank what he'd been planning to buy his mother. But then he remembered that Frank had been coming to church recently, so he said, "I was going to buy her a new translation of the New Testament—at the Christian bookstore."

Frank shrugged. "Okay, I've got money. Come on."

David still hesitated. "I don't know, Frank. I—I'd kinda rather buy her present with my own money. I've been working for it, saving it, and I wouldn't feel right if I let you buy the present."

Frank's expression hardened. "Look, do you want to be my friend or not?"

David looked at Seth, frowning, then slowly turned back to Frank. "Well, you see," he said with some embarrassssment, "my father let me work for the money, and he told me that was the way I was supposed to get my mother a present. He said it would mean more to me if I worked for it."

"Oh, he won't care," Frank said impatiently. "Look at it like this: I'm saving you money. You can spend the money you saved on something *you* want."

David sighed. "Okay," he said. "And—thanks." He and Seth pedaled slowly in first gear as Frank walked briskly between them toward the bookstore.

"In everything you do, put God first, and he will direct you and crown your efforts with success" (Prov. 3:6).

Discussion Questions:
1. Are all temptations obviously evil or wrong? Is Satan interested in getting us away from God one "tiny" step at a time? What was wrong with David's decision to let Frank buy his mother's gift?

2. Think back over the things you've done this past week. In how many of them did you put God first? What difference might it have made if you had put God first?
3. In what way will God "crown" our efforts with success if we put Him first? Does the Scripture quoted above mean *everything* we do will be successful?

Day 2

Frank's House

"Wow, that's a big pool!" David exclaimed, staring at the deep, clear water. It was the only private pool in the neighborhood, and he'd often wished he could swim there.

Frank dived in and swam to the other end. "Come on!" he called.

David whooped and did a cannonball dive. Seth followed right behind.

They swam until supper time. Then, Seth dressed and went home. David also began to get ready to leave.

"You don't have to go now, do you?" Frank asked, drying off with one of the thick towels stacked on a poolside table. "Come see my room first. You can call your parents from there and tell them you'll be late. And if you can stay," he added eagerly, "I'll fix us something to eat in the microwave."

David unfolded a towel and began to dry off. "Your parents aren't home?" he asked, following Frank into the house.

"Naw," Frank said casually. "They don't get home until 6:30 or later." He grinned as David followed him across the den, staring at the huge television and all the furniture and knickknacks. Frank pointed to the bookcase along one wall. "Those trophies are my step-father's. He was a star quarterback in college. He tried out with the Cleveland Browns, but he said his career as a lawyer was more important than playing pro ball."

"Wow," David murmured. He stumbled where the thick carpet ended and he began crossing the kitchen. Still gazing around he added, "I've never seen so many appliances!"

Frank laughed. "Yeah, well, they make my mom's life easier."

They went out a doorway into what once had been a double garage. Now, it was a huge bedroom—complete with a pool table, color TV, video game console, water bed, and so much athletic equipment that David thought he was in a sporting goods store. "All this stuff is yours?" he asked. "By yourself?"

"Uh-huh," Frank said, throwing his towel into one corner and pulling a fresh shirt and jeans from the closet. "Look around; play with anything you want to," he said, dressing.

David dropped his own clothes on the carpet and began dressing slowly, staring around at all the exciting things. He was most attracted to a tabletop slot car track along the front wall near the outside door. When he was dressed, he went to the track, set a car in one of the slots, and picked up the control. It wouldn't work.

Frank came up behind him. "You have to clean the contacts," he said. "I hardly ever use it anymore, so the contacts corrode."

While David was working on the car, he said, "You've got your own door—and your room's next to the kitchen. Neat."

"Sure," Frank laughed. "That way I can feed myself whenever I get hungry, and I can come and go as I please."

David laughed and set the car down. "You've got *everything*, don't you?"

Frank looked around the room, then back at David. "Yeah," he said with a laugh, then added, "or at least that's what my stepfather keeps telling me." The look he gave David made the younger boy wonder what Frank was holding back, what he was *not* saying.

"Then Jesus said to his disciples, 'It is almost impossible for a rich man to get into the Kingdom of Heaven'" (Matt. 19:23).

Discussion Questions:
1. Do you think Frank really has "everything"? Does he actually believe he has "everything"? What might Frank not have that he really wants?
2. How would Jesus likely "rearrange" Frank's parents' thinking?
3. Why did Jesus say, "It is almost impossible for a rich man to get into the Kingdom of Heaven"? What connection is there between that statement and the one from yesterday, that we must "In everything ... put God first"? What *would* make it possible for a wealthy person to be a follower of Jesus Christ?

Day 3

The Offer

"No!" David cried. He stared with shock at Frank.

Frank laughed and leaned against the racetrack. "Look, there's nothing wrong with doing that. Or maybe you're still a baby."

"There *is* something wrong with—with—"

"I told you, my parents won't be home for another hour—and I'll give you anything you want in this room."

David shook his head vigorously. "My father said I was never, *never* to do that, and I don't care what you offer me!"

"You've already done one thing today your father told you not to do, so what difference would one more make?"

"Is that what you want a friend for?" David asked, frowning. "Is that why you don't have any friends now?"

"Who says I don't have any friends?" Frank demanded, stiffening.

"My sister says so," David snapped. He hurried toward the door which opened onto the driveway. "And you can keep the present you bought for my mother!" He opened the door, gave Frank a final glare, and stalked out. As he reached the sidewalk he began running toward home.

Lori saw David slip into his room, and she noticed his troubled look. She stepped into his room and closed the door quietly behind her. "What's wrong?"

David looked at her with confusion and embarrassment—as if she had caught him doing something wrong. "Nothin'," he mumbled.

"Come on, you can't fool me. What have you been up to?"

He glared at her, his blue eyes the same shade as hers but tinged with fright. "Frank Rothman tried to—tried to buy my friendship."

She gave a knowing look. "Did you go swimming with him?"

"Yeah."

"And did he—try to do something else with you?"

42

David looked surprised. "Yeah. How'd you know?"

"Now you know why he doesn't have any friends." Her expression was filled with disgust. "He's messed up in the head."

David sat on the edge of his bed and plunged into thought. In a moment he looked at Lori and said, "I feel sorry for him. He wants a friend so—so desperately!"

"Well, he has strange ways of getting one," Lori said sourly. "You ought to hear what the guys on the football team say about him."

David sighed. "I'll bet." He looked earnestly at her. "It's like he knows everything wrong about love and nothing right about it."

Lori laughed gently and sat beside her brother. She put one arm around his shoulders. "That's why I love you, David; even when someone does something bad to you, you still try to love them and help them. I wish I could forgive as easily as you do."

"Where could we start—for helping Frank, I mean?"

She drew back. "Don't get me involved with him!" She laughed and reached for the Bible that was near David's bed. She thumbed through it looking for a passage. "Here's something you could talk to him about." She held her finger on the verses.

David glanced at her with some embarrassment. "Do you think I should tell Daddy about what Frank—?"

"Didn't you handle it okay? I mean, you knew what to do, didn't you?"

"Sure. I told him flat out it was wrong."

"Then I wouldn't stir up a fuss over it. If you want to help Frank, the right thing to do probably is to try to teach him what love really is. And maybe this is a place to start." She began to read:

" 'So don't worry at all about having enough food and clothing. Why be like the heathen? For they take pride in all these things and are deeply concerned about them. But your heavenly Father already knows perfectly well that you need them, and he will give them to you if you give him first place in your life as he wants you to' " (Matt. 6:31-33).

Discussion Questions:

1. Why do you suppose David said about Frank, ". . . he knows everything wrong about love and nothing right . . ."? What doesn't Frank seem to know about love? How might the above Scripture verses get him started on the right path about love?
2. What were several things David did *right* in today's chapter?
3. What evidence is there that God is at work in Frank Rothman's life? What evidence is there that Satan also is at work in his life?

Day 4

The Second Offer

"Hello, Frank," David said into the telephone receiver. "Have you still got that New Testament we bought for my mother?"

There was a long pause before an almost suspicious voice said, "Yeah."

"May I come over and look at it with you?"

"Look at it? Why?"

"I want to show you something in it."

There was another long pause before Frank answered, "Okay."

In minutes, David had ridden his bike to Frank Rothman's house. Frank seemed reluctant as he opened his bedroom door to let David in.

"You're not still mad at me?" Frank asked.

David grinned at him. "No."

"You—uh, you didn't tell anyone about—"

"Don't worry about it," David said. "C'mon, show me that New Testament."

Frank retrieved the bookstore sack from his pool table and handed David the slim book. David found Matthew 6:31-34 and read the verses, ending with, " 'So don't be anxious about tomorrow. God will take care of your tomorrow too. Live one day at a time.' "

Frank had sat at his desk and was leaning one elbow on it, his cheek on his open hand. "Do you want to take that with you when you leave?"

David looked a bit surprised as he closed the book. "Do you have another Bible?"

"No," Frank said, looking at the stuff piled on his desk. When he looked back at David, his eyes were hard, sarcastic. "Aren't you going now—now that you have what you came for?"

David's shoulders slumped. "I thought maybe I could be your friend."

Frank sneered. "I'm too busy to be friends with little kids." He spread one hand over the textbooks on his desk. "You see, my step-father wants me to work ahead of my class so I can skip a grade." He gave David a cold stare. "I'm smart enough to do that, you know."

"Your stepfather loves you?" David asked quietly.

Frank bristled. "Of course he does! My parents love me a lot—more than yours do, I'll bet!" He looked back at the papers and books on his desk. "Now go on, get out of here. I've got work to do."

"I'll leave this," David said, placing the New Testament on Frank's bed. "You might also read John 3:16—about how much God loves you."

Frank stood angrily. "Look, kid, stop trying to be like Josh and Chris and talking me into coming to church again. I didn't get anything out of it—except bored."

David shrugged and grinned sadly. "Well," he awkwardly began, "if you ever need a friend, you know where I am. And if you ever need love—more love than you've imagined—you can read in that book how to get it." He nodded to the New Testament. When Frank said nothing, David silently left.

" 'My sheep recognize my voice, and I know them, and they follow me. I give them eternal life and they shall never perish. No one shall snatch them away from me, for my Father has given them to me, and he is more powerful than anyone else, so no one can kidnap them from me' " (John 10:27-29).

Discussion Questions:
1. What decision did Frank make? To what did he say, "No"? To what did he, in effect, say, "Yes"?
2. In comparison with our human friends, what kind of friendship does Jesus offer us? How can we have Him as a real, day-to-day friend?
3. If we put God first in our lives, how can He influence or change our human friendships? How is David Matthews different from the non-Christians Frank Rothman knows?

Day 5

Meet Me Halfway

"Hello, David?" a quiet, sad voice on the telephone asked a few nights later. "This is Frank. Could I see you?"

"Sure. Do you want me to come to your house?"

After a few seconds of silence, Frank said, "No, I'll meet you half-way—under the street light by Mrs. Wards' house."

David hung up and asked his mother if he could go out. She said he could, so he hurriedly left and ran up the street toward Mrs. Wards' home. When he reached it, he smiled to himself, thinking of the sacks of aluminum cans he and Seth Jensen had collected with her so she could pay her utility bills. He heard footsteps running through the darkness, and he squinted toward them. Frank emerged from the gloom and stopped near him.

"Is something wrong?" David asked.

Frank bent over until he caught his breath; then, with quiet anger, he said, "I've had a fight with my stepfather. But I don't want to talk about that. I want to ask you something."

"Sure."

"Do you really want to be my friend?"

"Yeah," David said.

"And you don't want *anything*—not even to go swimming in my pool?"

"Right," David said, holding back the excitement he felt swelling up inside himself. "And if you do try to give me anything, I won't take it. But if you want to do things together, like go swimming, that's all right with me—as long as they're good things for friends to do."

Frank nodded. Frowning, he asked, "Another thing—were you for real when you said God loves *me*?"

David took a deep breath and slowly exhaled. "Well, I can tell you He does, and the Bible can tell you—but you won't *know* it until you let God begin to run your life."

46

Frank hung his head and muttered, "I get the idea it's a choice between God and—and the way my parents live."

David felt confused; He didn't want to encourage Frank to rebel against his parents, but he knew Jesus was calling him. Cautiously, he said, "God wouldn't want you to run away from them or anything like—"

"No, that's not what's bothering me," Frank said impatiently. He sighed, then smiled to show he was not mad at David. "I mean, I'm sort of like one of their *things.* They've got me for a son, in the same way that they've got Oldsmobiles and TVs and a pool. They feed me and buy me things—like I was a washing machine that needs soap and repairs."

David suddenly understood, and he felt like crying for Frank. From his spirit came the words, "Follow Jesus, Frank. He's got more love than either of us can understand. And He expects His followers to obey Him, which means obeying His law of love—*real* love."

"I think I want to make that choice," Frank said thoughtfully. "Last night I read in that New Testament that we have to choose between God and money. My parents—my mom and my step-father—have chosen money. That's the only thing they think about—how to get more and keep more." He paused, frowning, and David watched him intently. "I've only been to church three or four times," Frank resumed slowly, "and I don't really understand much of what your preacher is talking about. But I *know* I'm about to go crazy because of the way things are at my house." He looked as if he were about to cry, but he straightened and tried to look tough. "I also know that you're the only person who cares what happens to me. So if you say it's because of Jesus, then I want to follow Him too."

"It's because of Jesus," David said, grinning and wiping his eyes with the back of one hand. He laughed with nervous excitement. "You're okay, Frank. You know that?"

Frank grinned sheepishly. "No, I didn't. But anyhow—thanks for being my friend." He stuck out his right hand.

David shook Frank's hand with both of his.

"See you later," Frank said, turning to run back up the street.

"Yeah," David called. "See you!"

" *'You cannot serve two masters: God and money. For you will hate one and love the other, or else the other way around. So my counsel is: Don't worry about things...'* " (Matt. 6:24-25a).

47

Discussion Questions:
1. How has Frank Rothman changed? What caused him to change?
2. In what ways has David been a friend to Frank?
3. Read Romans 13:9-10. How do these verses apply to David's and Frank's situations?

WEEK FOUR

"I Hate Him!"

Day 1

"Hypocrites"

Mr. Rothman was standing with his back to the bookcase, which was filled with his trophies and law books. Mrs. Rothman, anxiously fingering her frosted brown hair, was seated at one corner of the sectional sofa. Frank, hands stuffed in his pockets, was hunched at the corner of the sofa farthest from her.

"We just want the best for you," Mr. Rothman said after a lull in the argument that had been raging like a forest fire. "All I've ever wanted for you is for you to be happy."

"And out of the way," Frank snapped, flicking a glare at him.

"Out of the way?" Mr. Rothman echoed in disbelief. He looked at his wife, then back at Frank. "*I'm* the one who's tried to involve you in my activities since your mother and I got together. I took you fishing—and you dropped overboard a two hundred dollar rod and reel. I took you to the Cowboys game, and you knocked my drink over in my lap. And then there was that trip—"

"The only reason you ever were nice to me," Frank said sullenly, "was to get Mom to like you."

"That's nothing but jealousy!" Mr. Rothman huffed, taking two steps toward Frank. He leveled a forefinger at the boy. "Little boy loses Mommy and won't forget it."

"Sy," Mrs. Rothman said in a pleading tone. Her face was twisted in a look of sympathy—for both her son and her husband. "Please, let's stop this fighting. Can't we just forget—"

51

"No, we can't," he snapped, glancing at her, then glaring at Frank. "We've avoided talking about this long enough, and I'm tired of him failing in everything he tries to do."

"Everything *you* push me into doing," Frank blurted. "And the only reason I've kept from talking about this is that I figured I'd better keep my mouth shut or you'd stop buying me all that—that *junk* you use to keep from having to really love me!" He folded his arms and scowled at Sy.

"Junk," Sy Rothman said, slumping with an incredulous expression. "Junk!" He spread his arms as if appealing to the ceiling for help. "If that's all it is to you—"

"It is! It's nothing but your way of buying me off, you—you adulterer!" Frank stormed as he leaped to his feet.

Sy whirled and slapped Frank across the face so hard the youth was knocked back onto the sofa.

Crying, Frank held his cheek and spat out, "That's all you are, and the Bible says you are—*God* says you are. And what's more, you're hypocrites! You accuse me of failing, of doing bad things, of being stupid, but it's *you* who are disobeying!"

His mother now stood, one hand to her mouth, tears streaming down her face. "Sy, make him stop. Make him take back—"

Mr. Rothman was already in motion, jerking off his belt and moving toward Frank—who scrambled over the back of the sofa, ran into his room, and burst outside through his door. In seconds he was gone, running madly down the sidewalk into the night.

"Then [Jesus] added, 'Now go away and learn the meaning of this verse of Scripture, "It isn't your sacrifices and your gifts I want—I want you to be merciful." For I have come to urge sinners, not the self-righteous, back to God' " (Matt. 9:13).

Discussion Questions:
1. When we sin, what does God—Christ—want us to do about it?
2. If you were with Frank right now, what would you say to him? If you were with Mr. Rothman, what would you say to him? And if you could talk to Mrs. Rothman, what would you tell her?

Day 2

"I Hate Them"

Frank gradually slowed his pace after running several blocks toward downtown. He had made a vague plan for buying a bus ticket and going to his grandmother in Missouri, but he finally realized he had only six or seven dollars in his pocket. He began thinking of what else he could do, where else he could go, and his pace became slower and slower. Finally, he turned into the park behind the elementary school and sank down on a bench.

When his thoughts and breathing began returning to normal, he became aware of a faint, sobbing sound nearby. Seeing no one, he began walking toward the sound. As he rounded a huge live oak tree, he saw a child huddled in the shadow of the tree's trunk. He knelt by the person and put one hand on his back. The child flinched and turned, exposing his face to the light of a street lamp.

"Say, aren't you Randy Dobbs—Chris' little brother?" Frank asked gently.

Sniffling, Randy nodded and wiped his nose. " 'Lo, Frank," he mumbled, trying his best to act as if he hadn't been crying.

"What's wrong with you?" Frank asked, forgetting his own troubles for the moment.

"They're mean to me," Randy said bitterly, "and they don't like me!" His chest jerked as he tried hard to stop crying. Frank smiled sadly and laid his arm on the boy's shoulders.

"It'll be okay," Frank assured him, patting his back. Randy sagged against him for a moment, then struggled to lean back against the tree trunk. He swabbed his cheeks with both fists angrily.

"Nope, it won't be okay. I've run away. They hate me, and I hate them! I'm not going back, so don't try to talk me into it!" He stood, ready to escape if Frank tried to make him go home.

Frank sat on the ground, raised his knees, and hooked his arms around them. "Can you tell me what happened?"

"They—they never pay any attention to me," Randy said in a rush. "Chris is the oldest, so he gets to do what he wants to, and Emilie is the baby, so they think everything she does is cute. But me—they forget about me."

"Hurts, doesn't it?"

Randy stopped sniffling and stared at Frank. "You know?" When he saw Frank nod, he slid down the tree trunk into a sitting position. "How come, with all your money and stuff, *you* know?"

Frank laughed bitterly. "I'll tell you what: I'll take your brother and sister and parents, and you can have all the stuff my parents buy me."

"Really?" Randy asked in wonderment. "But, how come?"

Frank laughed again, more lightly. " 'Cause you're *with* your parents; I've seen you all going to church, looking happy together. Me—I hardly ever see my parents. They're always working, even on Sundays."

"Even Sundays?" Randy exclaimed. He was silent for a while, then said, "Sundays, and Saturdays too, we—" Remembering he was mad, he stopped and said nothing more. Finally Frank stood. Randy stood with him, and without a word they began walking slowly toward Randy's house.

They met his father coming up the middle of a street, a flashlight glaring in one hand. Mr. Dobbs saw Randy and ran to him. He knelt and looked him over, then hugged him tightly. "Randy, we were so worried!"

"He thought you didn't love him," Frank quietly explained. "He thought you hated him—and that he hated you."

Mr. Dobbs glanced at Frank, then firmly grasped Randy's shoulders. "Are we all searching the neighborhood, calling everybody we can—including the police—because we *hate* you?"

"No—sir," Randy said, sniffing and beginning to cry again.

In a softer tone, Mr. Dobbs asked, "Have we been ignoring you again, not listening to you, not letting you snuggle with us while we're watching television?"

Randy solemnly nodded several times.

Mr. Dobbs picked him up, held him tightly, and began carrying him home. As they left Frank alone in the dark street, Mr. Dobbs said to Randy, "Well, we'd better start making up for that right now, hadn't we?" Randy giggled and put his arms around his father's neck.

" *'And how does a man benefit if he gains the whole world and loses his soul in the process? For is anything worth more than his soul?'* " (Mark 8:36-37).

Discussion Questions:
1. What trade did Frank offer Randy? Why did Frank make that offer? Why do you suppose Randy didn't accept the trade?
2. How does the Scripture quoted from Mark apply to the Rothmans? How does it apply to the Dobbses?
3. Explain what you think this means: "Things feed the body, but love feeds the soul."

Day 3

A Place

I can't go home, Frank miserably thought, *but I've got to have a place–any place–to stay.* He wished more than anything that he could find a place where somebody, anybody, would care for *him.*

Without realizing in which direction he had been walking, he saw that he was near David Matthews' house. A light was burning in one of the front rooms, a light that to Frank seemed inviting. *But what if they laugh at me–or just send me home?* he worried, stopping at the curb.

His desire for a friendly place was stronger, however, than his fears. He straightened and tried to look like the fourteen-year-old football player he was supposed to be. He went up the walk and rang the doorbell.

Mr. Matthews opened the door and turned on the porch light. "Oh—Frank," he said, slightly surprised. The two stared at each other silently.

Frank didn't know how to begin and was about to whirl and run, when Lori and David came up behind their father to see who was at the door. Together they said, "Frank!" David added, "What's wrong?"

Ashamed, and trembling inside, Frank managed to say, "Had another fight with my stepfather."

Mr. Matthews—a tall, brown-haired man with blue eyes—pushed open the screen door. "Why don't you come inside?" he asked.

"Yes—sir," Frank said, shyly following Lori and David into the family den.

"We were making hot chocolate," Lori informed him. "Would you like a mug?"

"That'd be nice," he mumbled, glancing at Mrs. Matthews, who had just entered the room. She smiled at him, and he sighed, stifling an unexplainable urge to run into her arms.

She, however, read his thoughts better than perhaps he did. With-

56

out saying a word, she went to him—a boy she had only seen and heard about—and took him in her arms. While David and Lori stared at them and at each other, and Mr. Matthews leaned on a kitchen counter in amazement, Mrs. Matthews stroked Frank's head as he broke into sobs.

"I'll call his parents," Mr. Matthews quietly said. "Maybe he can stay here for a while."

Mrs. Matthews led Frank into a corner of the den and sat with him where the others wouldn't stare. Frank let her hold him again as he barely heard Mr. Matthews speaking into the telephone: "Yes, he's here—Yes, I realize it's none of our business—Yes, I realize he's not our son or our problem, but—but—" Frank heard him sigh, as if struggling for patience. Then, in a soft but very firm voice, he said, "If you would just let him stay here for a while—maybe tonight?" After a moment, he added, "Yes, all right. We'll see that he gets to school tomorrow—Yes, I'll call you."

When he hung up, Frank let out the breath he'd been holding and sagged against Mrs. Matthews, crying as he had done only once before in his whole life: when his parents' divorce was final.

"'Worship the Lord alone. But if you are unwilling to obey the Lord, then decide today whom you will obey. . . . as for me and my family, we will serve the Lord'" (Josh. 24:14c, 15a & c).

Discussion Questions:
1. In what way did Mrs. Matthews answer Jesus' "love call"?
2. Whom—and what—would you say the Rothmans have decided to obey and serve? Whom, and what, would you say the Matthewses have decided to obey and serve? What difference does each family's decision seem to make in their lives?
3. Why do you suppose Frank would let a stranger hold him, and why wouldn't he be ashamed of crying with her?

Day 4

God's Glue

After school the next day, Frank went home with Lori and David. To Frank's surprise, fear and embarassment, Mr. Matthews had come home from work early—with a visitor Frank was too ashamed to look at: Pastor Burton. Mr. Burton led Frank into the living room and waited until the Matthewses had gone elsewhere. Then he smiled at Frank.

"None of my business, is it?" he began as he leaned against the back of the couch.

Frank squirmed, eyeing his fingernails as he cleaned each one nervously.

"Figure I'm going to preach at you?"

Frank glanced up and stifled an urge to grin. "I don't know," he shrugged. "I guess so."

Pastor Burton sighed and looked out the front bay window. Frank eyed him with caution. "Divorce is never right," the pastor said in a voice that seemed neither condemning nor approving. "It's against God's law and His wishes, because He wishes—desires—the very best for us; and a complete family unit is the best situation for us because in a family we learn about Him and we share His love with one another." He glanced at Frank. "Your turn."

Frank hesitated, but Pastor Burton remained silent. Frank cleared his throat, continued to pick at his fingernails, and said, "I hated my mother for getting a divorce. But I also felt—guilty."

Pastor Burton waited to make sure Frank was finished, then said, "Okay. But now she's remarried. What was won't ever be again. What are you going to do about it?"

Frank's thoughts spun and whirled—over his hours of anger and frustration at not being able to keep his real parents together, and over his jealousy and hatred toward his stepfather. *Yes*, he thought, *I am jealous. I thought at least if my dad couldn't have her, that I could, and that I could be the man of the house.* He sighed and felt his anger slip away from him. "I guess I'll just have to deal with it—with them—him."

"All right," Pastor Burton said, raising one knee and clasping his hands around it as he again gazed out the front window. "That's pretty much the way God feels about it. He wanted something better, but He'll deal with what is." Again, he waited, listening and glancing at Frank.

"How?"

"First, you've got to understand that no matter what has happened, God still loves you and all your parents just as much as He ever has—so much that He gave His son to die for us that we might be forgiven and come back to God—clean." He waited for Frank to absorb that statement, then said, "Second, God always is ready to forgive people when they turn around from their selfish ways and give Him control of their lives. He won't make us turn around; we have to do that. But then, because Jesus gave His blood as payment for what we do wrong, God can adopt us as His children, clean us up, and make us right."

Inwardly, Frank steamed. "Even adulterers?" he snapped.

"Are you any better?"

Frank prepared to spit out a bitter, angry answer, but he searched the pastor's face and saw no condemnation. After several moments, he lowered his eyes and said, "No. No, I'm not."

"Third," Pastor Burton resumed, "God will work through binding relationships—like your mother's new marriage—to bring about what He wants, which is a loving family. Her new marriage, and your new father, may be less than ideal, but your family can be blessed and made holy—clean and set apart from sin—by God's forgiveness and by the glue of His love!"

"And what am I supposed to do?" Frank asked sullenly.

Firmly, and with a kind and understanding gaze, Pastor Burton said, "Obey and love your stepfather and your mother. Confess your sins and be forgiven. Follow Christ."

Frank felt so overwhelmed that he laughed with surprise and disbelief. "Just like that!?" he asked, snapping his fingers. "Just—" He stopped when he realized that Mr. Burton was serious. He felt as if he were walking along a totally dark tunnel and had suddenly seen a bright light ahead at the end.

"Then Jesus stood up again and said to her, 'Where are your accusers? Didn't even one of them condemn you?'

" 'No, sir,' she said.

"And Jesus said, 'Neither do I. Go and sin no more'" (John 8:10-11).

Discussion Questions:
1. What does love have to do with forgiveness?
2. Why doesn't God *make* Frank and his parents—and people like them—do what He wants them to do?
3. What do you think Frank will do about his situation? What should the King's Kids do to help him?

Day 5

"Please...."

The Matthewses watched Frank and Pastor Burton go down the walk to the pastor's car. David whispered to Lori, "We gotta get the King's Kids together. Pray—you know?"

Lori nodded as her father put one arm around her shoulders and closed the door with his free hand.

At the Rothman's house, Mr. Rothman practically jerked open the door. He glanced at Pastor Burton, then glared at Frank. "Well, what have you got to say for yourself? And who's this? A cop?" He gave Pastor Burton a hard look as he opened the screen door for Frank. He grabbed Frank by one arm and pulled him inside. "Well?"

"I'm Jack Burton, pastor of the—"

"We don't need any, thank you," Mr. Rothman said as he slammed the door. He led Frank into the den where Mrs. Rothman stood, scarcely breathing. He turned to face his stepson.

Frank took a deep breath and let it part way out. "Please," he began hesitantly, looking from Sy to his mother and back, "I'm sorry." He took another deep breath. "I'm sorry I said all those bad things to you, and I'm sorry I've caused so much trouble." He lowered his eyes, remembering what Pastor Burton had said in the car coming home. "Will you forgive me?" he asked, trembling inside with a war between anger and a desire to make things right.

"Well, my goodness," Mr. Rothman said with an air of disbelief. He looked at his wife. "I never thought I'd hear that." He turned back to Frank. "Did that preacher convince you you were wrong?"

Frank struggled to control the anger he felt pushing up like lava in a volcano. "No, sir," he said, looking at his stepfather squarely. "But," he added with a rush of words, "I want God to take me and clean me up and give me a family to love; and I can't start that until I get things worked out here."

While his stepfather stared speechlessly, his mother broke as if

61

from a trance and came quickly to him. With hesitation, she reached out. Frank stepped to her, and they stiffly embraced. After a moment, they parted and looked at Mr. Rothman, who was watching them with an expression that seemed to be shifting between bewilderment and longing—and something Frank thought might be fear.

"I—um, I—forgive you," Mr. Rothman said indistinctly. Uncertain of what to do next, he added, "Want something to eat? Or how about a drink? Boy, I could sure use one!"

"Here are my directions: Pray much for others; plead for God's mercy upon them; give thanks for all he is going to do for them. Pray in this way for kings and all others who are in authority over us, or are in places of high responsibility, so that we can live in peace and quietness, spending our time in godly living and thinking much about the Lord" (1 Tim. 2:1-2).

Discussion Questions:
1. Talk about what Frank should do from now on. How do the above verses apply to him? Why should we pray even for unfair people in authority?
2. Why is Mr. Rothman so shaken by Frank's apology? What should Frank do to gain his stepfather's confidence?
3. What has Frank Rothman learned recently? What are some things he yet has to learn? (Read 2 Corinthians 10:4-5 and discuss how those verses might contain part of what Frank could learn.)

WEEK FIVE

New Life

Day 1

Spring

Football season ended with the Super Bowl, and when it was over, Frank's father seemed to forget that Frank had failed to become a star quarterback. Frank, with that pressure gone, began to notice things.

First, he noticed that spring was coming rapidly. Daffodils were sweeping yellow thickly across bare, brown flower beds, and trees everywhere were budding. Frank also began noticing Denise Kibler.

He had the picture in his mind that she was a tall, skinny girl with stringy blond hair and a sullen look that said she always was ready to fight. But one day as the "A" lunch students were racing down the long hall to the cafeteria, Frank saw an entirely different Denise. In fact, he bumped right into her.

Embarrassed that several of the popular kids had seen his clumsiness, he stopped to apologize to Denise. He then saw her soft, well-brushed, blond hair, and her friendly brown eyes and gentle face. He blushed and said, "I–I, uh, I'm sorry."

"That's okay," she said casually, moving on down the hall.

He stood rooted where he was, gazing at her.

After school, he was waiting. He had asked around and learned that she was not going with anyone. He had written her a note, but he hadn't found a way to pass it to her, so he waited outside when the bell rang. When she came out the front doors and he saw the wind and sunlight catch her hair, he suddenly lost his voice. She almost passed him before he could break loose from his trance.

"Say—say, Denise," he said as he stepped toward her, certain that he was croaking like a frog. Seeing several kids look at him, he went near her and almost whispered, "Walk you home?"

She nodded and lightly descended the steps, her hair flying gloriously behind her. Frank numbly followed.

In tense silence, he walked block after block, a little behind her and to one side. Thoughts swarmed in his head: *What can I say to her that she won't think is dumb? Should I ask to carry her books? No—that'd be dumb! Should I tell her I wrote her a note? No, she'd think that was stupid. Should I—* On and on it went. Now she was at her front door, facing him. He wished the ground would open at his feet and swallow him. He gulped hard.

"Want to come in?" she asked easily. "I'll get you a Coke."

"Sure," he rasped, then mentally kicked himself for sounding like some stupid seventh grader. He followed her inside, blushing.

Mrs. Kibler met him as he entered the kitchen. He hadn't seen her in a long time, and he was surprised to see that she was pregnant. He nodded and tried to smile, glancing from her to Denise and back. "Hi," he managed to say, still sounding like a frog. "I'm Frank Rothman."

"Yes, I know," Mrs. Kibler said, smiling. " I've seen you at church." She sat with some difficulty at the kitchen table. "Nice to see you again."

Silence followed, and Frank groped for something to say that wouldn't sound stupid. He stammered at last, "I, um, I see you're going to have another baby—a *new* baby, I mean."

Denise and her mother laughed quickly, looking at each other as if they shared a secret. Frank thought they were laughing at him. He said, "I mean, it's neat that Denise is going to have a baby brother—or sister."

"Yes, it is!" Denise said, handing him a glass of Coke and ice. He hardly looked at it. "Mom quit her job so she could give full-time care to her—or him. After all, any baby who's been dedicated to God since he—or she was conceived deserves the best care."

Frank took a sip from his glass—and dribbled the drink down his chin. He wiped it quickly, hoping his clumsiness hadn't been noticed, then said, "How can you already dedicate. . . ." He set the glass on a counter.

"God knows us in the womb long before we're born," Mrs. Kibler said softly. "So we decided, since God has restored our family and honored us with this gift," she patted her rounded midsection, "that we should give the child to Him."

Frank's thoughts suddenly were no longer on Denise; rather, they were on Mrs. Kibler's baby—and on his own childhood. "That's great," he said with a mixture of longing and unexpected happiness. He looked at Mrs. Kibler. "I really wish my parents had thought enough of me to do that."

"[Hannah, Samuel's mother, said,] 'I am the woman who stood here that time praying to the Lord! I asked him to give me this child, and he has given me my request; and now I am giving him to the Lord for as long as he lives'" (1 Sam. 1:26b-28a).

Discussion Questions:
1. How has Denise Kibler changed during the time Frank has known her? What do you think made the difference?
2. Why did the Kiblers dedicate their unborn child to God? What difference do you think that dedication might make in the child's life?
3. How do you think the Kiblers would feel about abortion? What might Mrs. Kibler say about it?

Day 2

His Children

All that evening and the next day, Frank thought about the Kibler baby. He was puzzled, and deeply hurt, that a baby not yet born could be loved more than he was. His bitterness toward his mother and stepfather increased, but he said nothing. And in school the next day, he found that he could hardly wait to see Denise—and maybe to go home with her again to see her mother. "God," he prayed silently several times, "I sure hope you let that baby be born normal!"

When the final bell rang, Frank hurried to the front entrance, his heart thumping like the footsteps of the kids around him. He stood at one side of the steps and tried his best to look cool. But other kids who glanced at him grinned to themselves—he looked like a worried stork with curly black hair. They grinned even more as they whispered among themselves, "The ex-quarterback weirdo likes the ex-fighter weirdo!"

But when Denise appeared, the other kids—and, indeed, the rest of the world—seemed to disappear for both her and Frank. " 'Lo," he said quietly, falling into step beside her. She glanced shyly at him and grinned. After they had walked a block and were away from the crowds of kids, he took her books—and gently took her right hand in his left hand; he fought back a whoop of excitement. She flashed a smile at him that he thought he'd never forget.

As they went up the walk to her front door, he cleared his throat and asked, "When's the baby due?"

"In about a month." She turned and took her books from him. "Want to come in?"

"Haven't got the time," he said, frowning slightly. "Since I had that big fight with my stepfather, he's stopped giving me money and makes me work when I come home after school. Today I have to clean our pool."

"Is that all that's bothering you?" she asked gently. His frown deepened, and he gave her a questioning look. She added, "I saw you twice today in school, and both times you were frowning." She ran one finger across his wrinkled forehead, and the frown disappeared as if by magic. He smiled sadly.

"I've been thinking that it's funny—not funny, but odd—that your new baby is loved more before he's even born than I'm loved now."

Denise straightened and her smile became radiant. "That may be true in a way, but in another way it's not true at all. When you get home—do you have a Bible?" He nodded, and she said, "When you get home, read 1 John 3:1-2. When my parents were separated last year, and my father was gone, Grandpa Wiggins showed me those two verses—they helped me a lot."

"First John 3:1-2, " Frank repeated. He sighed and smiled. "Well, see you tomorrow—I hope."

"You will!" she said gaily, pulling open the door.

Frank ran home and cleaned the pool as quickly, and thoroughly, as he could. He ate supper with a sense of excitement and could hardly wait to be excused from the table so he could go into his room and read the New Testament David had given him. He hurried to his room, found the book, and lay down on his bed. He found 1 John and began to read:

"See how very much our heavenly Father loves us, for he allows us to be called his children—think of it—and we really are! But since most people don't know God, naturally they don't understand that we are his children. Yes, dear friends, we are already God's children, right now, and we can't even imagine what it is going to be like later on. But we do know this, that when he comes we will be like him, as a result of seeing him as he really is" (1 John 3:1-2).

Discussion Questions:
1. How do we become a child of God? Before being saved, whose child are we? How can Frank become a child of God, and how can he *know* that he is God's child?
2. What difference in Frank's life do you think Denise will make—and has already made?

69

Day 3

Beginnings

Frank and Denise were slowly eating lunch in a corner of the cafeteria, away from most of the rest of the kids—who by now all knew that Denise and Frank were going together. Frank's and Denise's heads were close together, and their talk was so quiet that no one nearby could overhear them.

"I don't understand what you—what the Bible—means by saying that if we believe in Jesus, we become a brand new person inside," Frank said, almost whispering. "How can anything we can't see change something we can see? Take, for example, that strange kid that Seth Jensen and some of the others have seen hanging around the neighborhood. He looks so lost and helpless, but when we try to talk to him, he runs away. Could Jesus make him different?"

Denise laid one hand on Frank's hand that was nearest her. "Didn't you say I was really different from the way I was last year?"

Frank nodded enthusiastically.

"And didn't you say that you were already feeling different—as if you'd been going down a long, dark tunnel and suddenly could see light ahead?"

Again Frank nodded.

She took a bite of bread.

"So if I become a follower of Christ," Frank said, poking his fork at his uneaten green beans, "I get a chance to become new again, to start over?"

"Just like our baby," Denise said, grinning. "But with you, like with me, the Holy Spirit was working in your spirit even before you started thinking about becoming a Christian."

Frank smiled shyly. "You mean, maybe He brought you to me?"

"So you could see Him better," she added.

Frank straightened, feeling a thrill and a special warmth inside. He sensed that one way or another God was answering his unspoken prayer: that his empty life be filled with love. "I like you," he whispered to Denise.

Tears sprang into her eyes, and she whispered back, "I like you, too—but please don't send me any more notes. Janie gave me the last one in English class, and Mrs. Marder took it and read it out loud!"

They quickly finished eating. As they were leaving the cafeteria, Frank asked, "How long now?"

"Any day," Denise said, thinking of how her parents had been practicing breathing exercises together to make the delivery easier. "In fact, my mom's already packed to go to the hospital."

"When someone becomes a Christian he becomes a brand new person [a new creation] inside. He is not the same any more. A new life has begun!" (2 Cor. 5:17).

Discussion Questions:
1. What does Frank seem to have the most difficulty believing? What evidence does Denise use to help him believe?
2. Why is a "new beginning" important to Frank?

Day 4

Birth

Frank Rothman stood outside the viewing room of the hospital's maternity ward, his hands pressed against the thick glass. He gazed at an incubator. Inside it, covered with a light pink blanket, slept a form that seemed as precious to him as anything he'd ever seen.

"Beautiful, isn't she?" asked a soft voice behind him, startling him from his thoughts.

He turned and grinned at Denise. "Sort of—but how come she's all wrinkly and red?"

Denise laughed. "Silly. That's the way she's supposed to be."

"Oh," Frank said, turning back to stare at tiny Elizabeth Denise. "Why isn't she moving around?"

"She's sleeping. Wait till she gets hungry."

They walked down the long, strange-smelling hall to Mrs. Kibler's room. Mr. Kibler was sitting on the edge of his wife's bed, holding her hand. He greeted Frank, then looked back at his wife. "She's perfect," Frank heard him say quietly. "Just perfect."

"I know," Mrs. Kibler said, laughing. "I counted her fingers and toes and checked every inch of her. God gave us a perfect gift."

Soon, a nurse in cap and gown came in, holding a small bundle wrapped in pink. She frowned at Denise and Frank, but Mrs. Kibler quickly said, "Please, let them stay."

"They'll have to be masked and gowned—and so will your husband, if he's to stay."

"He is," Mrs. Kibler said.

When the young people and Mr. Kibler were properly dressed, the nurse gave the pink bundle to Mrs. Kibler. She began nursing it, and Frank felt a growing sense of excitement. When Elizabeth cooed slightly and lay back in her mother's arms, Mrs. Kibler put her over one shoulder and gently patted her back. The baby burped loudly; Frank chuckled behind his gauze mask. Mrs. Kibler then slowly climbed out of bed, and her husband reached slightly as if he were going to get the baby. But Mrs. Kibler went around the bed and stood before Frank, holding the baby toward him.

"Me?" Frank asked, feeling panicky that he would be offered anything so fragile and new. "You want me to hold her?"

Mrs. Kibler settled Elizabeth in his arms and showed him how to support her head in the crook of his left arm. Then she returned to the bed. Frank stared in amazement at the tiny face, much smaller than any face he'd seen. Hesitantly he pulled back the soft blanket so he could see her hands. He slipped one finger inside one of Elizabeth's closed fists, and she uncurled her fingers—then gripped his finger.

"Look, she's holding my finger!" he cried, ignoring the tears brimming his eyelids. He looked back down at her. "You're beautiful, did you know that? Simply beautiful!" Love sprang outward and upward from inside him. *Oh, Lord, is this baby like me—is this the way you feel toward me?*

"For unto us a Child is born; unto us a Son is given; and the government shall be upon his shoulder. These will be his royal titles: 'Wonderful,' 'Counselor,' 'The Mighty God,' 'The Everlasting Father,' 'The Prince of Peace.' His ever-expanding, peaceful government will never end" (Isa. 9:6-7a).

Discussion Questions:
1. Why do you suppose Mrs. Kibler gave Elizabeth to Frank instead of to her husband or Denise? In what way did Frank think that the baby was like him?
2. What wonderful mystery is there in the fact that God would come to us in the form of a baby, a human child? What connection is there between that fact and Jesus' teaching, "The meek and lowly are fortunate! for the whole wide world belongs to them" (Matt. 5:5)?
3. What could this mean: "Christ's love call can be heard in each baby's cry"?

Day 5

Ashes

Frank hardly could wait to get home and share his joy with his parents. But when he burst into the house, his mother was furious. "Where have you been?" she asked. "Didn't we tell you to come straight home after school?"

"I've been at the hospital," Frank said breathlessly, smiling despite the stern anger of his mother's expression. "Mrs. Kibler had her baby, and—"

"Change your clothes. Have you forgotten about the dinner party? The high school coach is going to be there, and your father wants you to make a good impression on him. Maybe you can make something out of yourself next year, if you make the junior varsity in tenth grade."

Frank fought back the anger and frustration he felt surging up inside. "But mother," he began, forcing his voice to remain calm, "don't you even want to hear about—"

"No," she said evenly, "I don't. You know that after your father and I divorced, I had that operation to make sure I'd never have another baby—so I don't want to hear about some other woman's child. Go change. Your stepfather will be home soon."

Frank felt as if his happiness had burned up like a scrap of paper, leaving him with only the taste of ashes in his mouth. But as he stared at his mother, he realized that his own unhappiness was nothing compared with hers. In her pained expression, Frank saw an emptiness and coldness that frightened him. Impulsively, he went toward her with the intention of hugging her tightly. Just before he touched her, however, she turned and walked quickly toward her room. "Hurry," she said.

"Yes, ma'am," Frank muttered, going to his own room.

He felt like crying, but he also felt angry. He felt frustrated, but for the first time, he also felt concerned about his mother's situation. The

74

hurt he felt for her was stronger than his disappointment over not being able to share his joy with her. *God, how can I help her?* he wondered desperately. *How can I help her to—to live again?* As he began changing clothes, his prayer kept running through his mind, and he wondered if God would answer him, even though he wasn't yet a Christian.

" *'Those who mourn are fortunate! for they shall be comforted'* " (Matt. 5:4).

Discussion Questions:
1. In what sense is Frank "mourning" for his mother? By whom are "mourners" comforted? How would being comforted make a "mourner" fortunate?
2. Do you think God will answer Frank's prayer, even though he isn't a Christian? In what way is he already a Christian?
3. In what ways has Frank changed?

WEEK SIX
The Enemy

Day 1

Shrinking

Mrs. Rothman's refusal to share Frank's joy hurt him perhaps more than he was willing to admit. He found himself once again becoming bitter and angry about little things, even though he tried harder than ever to keep up the happiness he'd recently found. But it was hard. It was as if he were shrinking spiritually.

One thing he decided to do was to give the Kibler baby a present. But even that seemingly simple idea turned into a hassle.

"No, I won't give you any money for a present," his father said across the dinner table on Monday night. "You said money isn't everything and things mean nothing to you, so why should I—why should *we*—give you anything?"

"Because you claim I'm your son, I guess," Frank said with quiet bitterness.

His father's glare hardened. "I don't claim anything. But I am responsible for you, and I'm responsible for seeing that you learn responsibility—which so far you've shown little sign of doing. If you want money, you earn it."

"All right, I will!" Frank snapped, throwing his napkin on the table and stalking into his room. He shut the door and sat down at his desk to think.

He was too young to get a job, he knew, and grass was not yet growing high enough for him to earn money mowing yards—even if his stepfather would let him use the mower for that. He ran over in his mind all the ways he knew kids could make money. Then he remembered that Seth Jensen and that old woman had been picking up aluminum cans. He dug a newspaper out of a stack of material he'd been using for a state history project and turned in it to an advertisement for a recycling center. *Twenty-eight cents a pound.* He wondered how many cans made a pound. Since it was still early in the evening, he quietly slipped out of his room and went to find Seth, who could tell him about can collecting.

Frank found Seth with David Matthews. They were playing baseball with a plastic bat and ball under a street light near Seth's house. Frank ran out for a fly ball with David and caught it just above the boy's head. He grinned and handed it to him. "Would'a conked you," he said.

"Naw, I had it," David said, grinning as he threw the ball back to Seth. "How're you doin'?" David asked Frank.

Frank shrugged, looking at the pavement. "Okay, I guess." As Seth approached, Frank glanced at him and asked, "Say, how many cans does it take to make a pound?"

" 'Bout twenty-one," Seth said, "depending on how thick each is. Why? You goin' into the scrounging business like us poor folks?"

Frank laughed and nodded. "I've been cut off from the 'good life,' " he said. "But I want to buy the Kiblers' baby a present, so I need to earn some money."

David and Seth looked at each other, then David said to Frank, "That sounds like a good idea. Can we help you?"

Frank frowned thoughtfully, then said, "No, I don't think so. I want to do this myself—you know, make it *my* gift."

David laughed slightly, and Frank was irritated by his laugh. David gently said, "Sure, Frank. We understand."

"You understand what?" Frank said defensively.

"We understand how you like to do things for yourself."

Frank looked from one boy to the other and still didn't understand why they were grinning at him. Irritated further, Frank walked away, head down. "See you," he mumbled.

"Yeah. Nice talkin' to you," Seth called, grinning to David as he ran back to his batter's position.

"And let us not get tired of doing what is right, for after a while we will reap a harvest of blessing if we don't get discouraged and give up. That's why whenever we can we should always be kind to everyone, and especially to our Christian brothers" (Gal. 6:9-10).

Discussion Questions:

1. What is Frank doing right but in the wrong way? What do Seth and David seem to understand about him that he doesn't yet understand about himself?
2. In what ways has Frank's life gotten harder since he began answering Jesus' love call? What could he do to make things easier on himself? Of what is he in danger?

Day 2

Working

For three days, after school and after finishing his chores at home, Frank walked the roads north of his neighborhood and at the edge of town. Carrying a vinyl garbage sack, he picked up all the cans he found. And as he walked, two thoughts often ran through his mind in different forms. The first thought was, *I feel stupid out here doing this; people driving by look at me like I'm some kind of bum—and I'm not; I've probably got a better house by far than they do!* The second thought was, *Seth and David probably wanted to help just so they could claim they had thought of giving Elizabeth a present—or so they could steer me away from the cans they help that old woman pick up.* The first thought was humbling, in a very unpleasant sort of way; the second thought increased his bitterness—and made him feel that he was shrinking still further. But he kept walking and picking up cans until his feet were sore and two garbage sacks were full of flattened cans.

The two lumpy sacks slouched in the storage shed at the back of Frank's yard. He looked at them and muttered, "Didn't know there were so many beer drinkers in the world." Tired, he trudged quietly into the house, avoiding any confrontation with his parents; he did not realize that they also were avoiding any confrontation, or even conversation, with him.

He went into his room and got out his pocket calculator. He switched it on. "Let's see," he murmured, "I'd guess twenty pounds per sack—that's forty pounds—times twenty-eight cents a pound—" He punched the numbers into the calculator. "That's eleven dollars and twenty cents." He leaned back in his chair with a sigh and a slight smile. "That oughta do it; I can buy a decent present with that much—and stop this stupid tromping through ditches, picking up smelly, sticky cans! Man, I never realized how bad beer stinks!" He switched off his calculator and put it back into his desk drawer.

He undressed and went to bed, thinking, *Eleven dollars in three days! That's not bad. Maybe I should just buy a five dollar gift and keep the rest....*

"*Notice among yourselves, dear brothers, that few of you who follow Christ have big names or power or wealth. Instead, God has deliberately chosen to use ideas the world considers foolish and of little worth in order to shame those people considered by the world as wise and great. He has chosen a plan despised by the world, counted as nothing at all, and used it to bring down to nothing those the world considers great, so that no one anywhere can ever brag in the presence of God*" (1 Cor. 1:26-29).

Discussion Questions:
1. In what ways is Frank being "brought down"? Why might it be God's will that this is happening to Frank? Is God being mean?
2. What are at least two of the temptations Frank, unknowingly, is facing? How have those temptations become stronger because he turned down Seth and David's help? If he continues to "shrink"— and gives in to his temptations—how might his life become harder still?
3. In the Scripture verses, what is the "plan despised by the world"?

Day 3

"Liars!"

Frank woke so late on Friday that he had to rush off to school without eating breakfast. That put him in such a bad mood that he hardly even spoke to Denise when he sat with her at lunch. She sensed his mood and said little, not wishing to make him angry. But he interpreted her silence as rejection, so he soon felt bitter and hurt, though he kept silent. Thus, when he went home he was in a foul mood. And what he found—or did not find—there sent him into a rage.

"Who took my cans?" he stormed, sliding back the patio door so hard that the thick glass quivered. His mother, who had just come home from work, was in no mood for anything but a drink and an hour's silence.

"How should I know?" she snapped. "And what cans are you talking—"

"The aluminum cans I collected to sell so I could buy a present. . . ," he fumed, then finally noticed her blank, exasperated expression. "Oh, never mind," he growled. "I think I know who stole them." He slammed out of the house and trotted toward David's and Seth's homes, which were near each other.

He found the boys in David's yard; they were flying paper airplanes. Frank deliberately stepped on David's plane as he stopped between the boys. David had bent down to pick up the airplane, but when he saw the look on Frank's face, he jerked backwards as if he had been rushed by a snarling dog.

"What'd you do with them?" Frank demanded, fists on his belt.

"With what?" David asked, getting set to run for the house.

"With the sacks of cans I'd picked up," Frank snarled, wanting nothing but an immediate confession and return of his property.

David looked at Seth, who shrugged. David gave Frank as honest a look as he could. "I don't know what you're talking—"

"Liars!" Frank stormed, interpreting David's look of frightened honesty as a look of guilt. He took a step toward the boy. "And I want them back—*now!*"

Seth began, "Frank, we don't have—" Frank whirled and struck him in the chest with his fist. Seth fell on his back. He clutched his chest in pain, fighting to get his breath.

David ran to his friend and knelt by him, then stared up at Frank angrily and exclaimed, "Listen! We didn't take your cans. We haven't even been near your house! Why would we steal them anyhow?" He turned to check Seth, who slowly sat up.

Frank sighed noisily. "You'd steal them to help that old woman, I guess," he said, suddenly noticing the pain in Seth's expression. But he would not move toward the boys.

"We wouldn't steal to help Mrs. Wards," David said firmly, giving Frank a cold stare. "And you might at least ask nicely before you go around slugging people smaller than you are!"

Frank suddenly felt shame, but he hid it. Frowning, he muttered, "I had two sacks of flattened cans in our storage shed, and last night someone stole them. If it wasn't you two, who was it?"

David thought a moment. "I don't know, Frank." Seth was breathing more easily, so David stood and helped him to his feet. "But if we help you catch the thief, will you promise not to hit him—or do something worse?"

"I don't need—" Frank said, then saw that the boys' expressions were filled with sympathy and a desire to help, despite the fact that Frank had hit Seth. Frank looked away. "I won't promise anything. Whoever stole my cans is my enemy, and my enemies had better *watch out!*" Even as he snapped out his threat, he heard the hollowness of it. He sniffed and shrugged—and glanced at David and Seth. "Do you really think you could help?"

" 'Under the laws of Moses the rule was, "If you kill, you must die." But I have added to that rule, and tell you that if you are only angry, *even in your own home, you are in danger of judgment! If you call your friend an idiot, you are in danger of being brought before the court. And if you curse him, you are in danger of the fires of hell'* " (Matt. 5:21-22).

Discussion Questions:
1. Why do you suppose Frank is angry so much of the time? Why is

anger condemned by Christ? Who, in a spiritual sense, is served by the kind of anger that Frank lets control him?

2. Who actually is Frank's enemy?

3. How did David deal with Frank's anger? How did Frank's mother deal with it? How could—or should—Frank deal with it?

Day 4

The Plan

Before dusk, David had called all the King's Kids. They quickly gathered at David and Lori's house, eager to hear what was up. Frank, by then, had settled down a lot, and he settled down completely when Denise came. She led him to one side of the den.

"Did you think I was mad at you?" she whispered as the others flocked to the kitchen for orange juice and soft drinks.

He slowly nodded, picking at his fingernails.

"I was just trying to stay out of your way," she explained. "Before my father accepted Jesus, he got mad a lot. I saw the same thing in you. He used to hit me when he was mad—taking his anger out on me, I guess. So when I saw you, I sort of hid from you—when I should have shown you the love Jesus has for you, even when you're mad."

Frank's gaze shot to her face. "Are you kidding?"

She shook her head, grinning, then leaned over and kissed him on the forehead. It was the first time she'd kissed him, and his anger melted like a chocolate bar on a hot day.

"All right, you two," Lori teased as she led the others into the den. They found places to sit, and David quickly explained what had happened to Frank's cans.

As David finished, he suggested, "How about setting a trap, like we did when the dogs were being poisoned?"

"How would we bait the trap?" Chris asked.

"We've got a sack of cans we were saving for Mrs. Wards," Seth said brightly. "How about letting Frank take them and put them in his storage shed?"

"How'll we know the thief will see him," Joshua asked, "and be brave enough to come back for more? Won't he be expecting trouble?"

"Maybe he—or she," Denise said thoughtfully, "is so desperate to steal anything worth selling that she, or he, will be hanging around."

85

Soon, Frank was on his way home with a sack of rattling aluminum cans. He practically threw them into the storage shed. He went toward the house, wanting to look around to see if the culprit was hiding somewhere in the vacant lots and fields to the north. But looking around might raise the thief's suspicions, so he controlled himself and went inside.

When darkness had fully come and Frank's parents had settled down to watch television, Frank slipped outside. Soon he heard a faint whistle—but he saw no one. He crept around to the back of his house, and thought he saw a dim shadow moving near the far left corner of their chainlink fence—and another shadow creeping along near the right corner. The whistle had assured him the shadows were friendly. So he settled down to wait.

Frank waited—and waited. His muscles were getting stiff, and he was starting to doubt that the plan would work. At last, he became sure that the thief hadn't seen him store more cans in the shed. He started to stand up, but then saw a dark figure haltingly coming toward the yard through the vacant lots. The dark, rather small figure ran—then stopped; ran—then stopped again. At the fence, the figure jumped up and over without making any noise. Into the shed it went, and a rattle of cans came through the still darkness.

Instantly four bright lights flooded into the shed, and eight King's Kids appeared, leaping the fence with lights in hand. The small figure burst from the shed at a dead run, but was grabbed by Joshua and Richard. They pinned him down while the others held their lights on what turned out to be—a very frightened little boy.

Frank broke through the circle of King's Kids, looked down at the boy, and rushed toward him with his fists doubled. "I'll teach you not to steal!" he yelled.

Joshua grabbed him by one arm and stopped him. When Frank resisted, Joshua held him even more firmly. "No," Joshua ordered. "David said you promised. You'll keep that promise—won't you?"

"Happy are the kind and merciful, for they shall be shown mercy" (Matt. 5:7).

Discussion Questions:
1. What would life be like if God were not merciful? What would our lives be like if we did not follow God's example and show mercy?
2. When someone hurts us, what is our *natural* instinct? How then could Jesus say, "*Happy* are the kind and merciful"? Does His statement mean we should not punish wrongdoers?
3. What should the King's Kids do with the thief?

Day 5

Decisions

"What'll we do with him?" Janie Warren asked, kneeling beside the little boy to get a closer look at his smudged and tearful face.

"Call the police," Sammy Fletcher declared.

"Yeah, let them take him to the juvenile home," Richard said.

"No," Chris said, remembering his own scrape with the law. "Let's find out who his parents are and call them."

"Who are you?" Joshua asked kindly, kneeling beside Janie. The boy was no longer being held down, but was still lying as if he were pinned. "What's your name?"

The boy said nothing. Instead, he looked from one of the King's Kids to another. What he saw and how he interpreted their expressions, none of them could tell. But he still looked terrified.

"What I want to know," Frank fumed, "is why you were stealing *my* cans! Did I ever do anything to you?"

The boy's head jerked slightly as he turned to look at Frank. He said nothing.

"Answer me, you little punk, or I'll bash you!" Frank said, shaking a fist near the boy's face.

Joshua pushed Frank's fist away and looked firmly at him. "You're not going to bash anyone."

Frank stood and squared off against Joshua, who slowly stood. The King's Kids backed away, aiming their lights toward the ground so any adults watching from windows couldn't see what was going on. Most of the kids thought it was about time someone like Josh taught Frank a lesson. Frank said in a threatening tone, "He stole from me, so I've got a right to make him pay—or at least to make him tell us where he's hidden the cans he stole."

"He should tell, but not because you beat him up," Joshua said calmly. "And he should be punished, but not with your fists."

"And why not?" Frank demanded, poised to throw a punch.

88

" ' "There is a saying, 'Love your friends and hate your enemies.'
But I say: Love your enemies!" '*—that's why," Joshua said, reaching
down to help the little boy stand. He turned his back to Frank and
placed his hands on the boy's shoulders to steady him. "What's your
name?" he asked again. When the boy didn't answer, Joshua said,
"Do you have a home?"

After a moment, the boy shook his head slightly.

"I didn't think so," Josh muttered. He began leading the boy to a
gate in the fence.

"What're you gonna do with him?" Frank called, almost in a
whine.

"Take him to my house," Josh answered without turning, "feed
him, clean him up—then find out where he belongs."

The other King's Kids followed Joshua out of the yard. The last
one, Denise, closed the gate behind her. He ran to the fence and
leaned on it. "But what am I supposed to do?" he yelled. "I want my
cans back!"

Josh's voice came back through the darkness: "Go read the verse
I quoted from Matthew 5—and have a good night!"

" *There is a saying, "Love your friends and hate your enemies."
But I say: Love your enemies! Pray for those who persecute you! In
that way you will be acting as true sons of your Father in heaven' "*
(Matt. 5:43-45a).

Discussion Questions:
1. In what way are anger, hate, and fear all alike? Whom do feelings
   like those help most?
2. Frank did what was natural—he hated his enemy and tried to like
   his friends. Joshua did what was *un*natural. How? What do you
   think was the Holy Spirit's part in what happened?
3. In what way does today's chapter illustrate the verse, " 'You cannot
   serve two masters: God and money. For you will hate one and
   love the other, or else the other way around' " (Matt. 6:24)? Whom
   did Joshua "serve"? Whom did Frank serve?

---

*Matt. 5:43-44a

A Home for Mark

Day 1

Uncertainty

"Who is *that?*" Mr. Wiggins asked as Joshua led the frightened, dirty little boy into the den of the Wiggins' home. "Where'd he come from?" He glanced at the other King's Kids filing into the house, then joined his wife and the kids in staring at the little boy. The stranger seemed to shrink under their looks.

Joshua sat on the couch with the boy. "We don't know who he is—he won't talk to us. We think he's from somewhere north of our subdivision. We've seen him hanging around near the clubhouse, and he's stolen some sacks of aluminum cans from Frank Rothman's house."

Janice Wiggins, standing in the hallway door with her arms folded, said, "Just call the police. They'll know what to do with him."

"Not yet," Joshua said, giving his parents a pleading look. "Couldn't we at least clean him up and feed him?"

"He looks like trouble," Janice muttered, and went back to her room.

Mrs. Wiggins joined Joshua and the boy on the couch. When she took one of his hands, she saw that it had been cut and bruised. She turned his face toward her and wet one finger to wipe some of the dirt away. Beneath the dirt, she saw bruises on his cheeks and under one eye. He trembled as she touched him, so she put one arm around him and drew him close.

"What's your name?" she asked quietly.

91

The boy said nothing and seemed to shrink even further into the couch.

"Who beat you up?" Joshua asked.

Still the boy said nothing.

"Whom do you live with?" Mrs. Wiggins said—with no response from the boy. She looked at her husband. "He's like an animal that's cornered but too scared to fight."

Mr. Wiggins came near the boy and bent down to look at him. "Well, I doubt that he's been living out in the open, even if he is dirty. He must have a home."

"Some home," Denise Kibler murmured from near the couch.

"Yes," Mr. Wiggins said thoughtfully. He straightened and sighed. "I suppose we'll have to call the county welfare department. They'll have social workers who can take care of him and find his parents."

"But he can stay here tonight, can't he?" Joshua asked anxiously, afraid his parents were going to take the boy somewhere immediately.

Mr. Wiggins smiled. "Yes, certainly. After all, if *I* were in his condition, I wouldn't want to be turned out." He looked at his wife. "Is there anything left from supper?"

"Do for others what you want them to do for you" (Matt. 7:12a).

Discussion Questions:
1. Frank, Joshua, Janice, and Mr. Wiggins each wanted to do something with—or to—the boy. With whose suggestion(s) would Jesus be pleased?
2. Compare the verse above (Matt. 7:12) with Matthew 25:35-40. How are the verses alike? How are they examples of Jesus' "love call"?
3. What risk, connected with helping the boy, did Janice Wiggins point out, and how would she have handled that risk? In what ways is it risky or possibly embarrassing to help people? How do you think Jesus would want us to deal with that risk or possible embarrassment?

Day 2

The Clean-up Campaign

While the little boy ate supper, all of the King's Kids except Denise and Joshua left. Denise watched with interest as Mrs. Wiggins served him and showed him how to use a napkin.

"How's that baby sister of yours?" Mrs. Wiggins asked. She cut the boy a piece of pie and piled ice cream on it.

"Oh, she's just fine," Denise said, smiling. "Mom and she came home from the hospital finally—and boy am I glad! Dad's a good father, but he's a terrible cook. If you and Mrs. Warren hadn't brought over those casseroles, we'd have eaten hamburgers every night."

"What's wrong with that?" Joshua wondered aloud.

After a moment's silence, Denise said, "I—I think it's great what you're trying to do for this kid. Not many people would be so giving—and loving."

"Please, don't tell anyone," Mr. Wiggins said quietly, watching the boy.

"Why not?" Denise wondered. "Are you afraid you'll get into trouble?"

"No . . . ," Mr. Wiggins said slowly, glancing at his wife. "But it's just better if it's done quietly."

Denise looked puzzled. "But—when the Lord brought my mom and dad back together, I couldn't wait to tell people what He'd done."

"That's different," Mr. Wiggins said. "When the *Lord* does something, we should brag—in a nice way, of course."

The boy handed Mrs. Wiggins his plate and silverware. Mrs. Wiggins put them into the sink and motioned for Joshua to wash them. She then led the boy down the hall, got a towel and wash cloth from a cabinet, and led him into the bathroom.

Denise grinned. "Bet he's not going to like that," she said.

"Don't you like to be clean?" Josh asked. "And sleep in fresh clothes on clean sheets in a warm bed?"

"Sure," Denise answered, "but he doesn't look like he's used to it. I figured he wouldn't like what he wasn't used to."

Mr. Wiggins gave an amused smile and asked, "Does being cleaned up feel funny for a while? Or are people like pigs: Even if you clean them up they go right back to wallow in their mud?"

Denise laughed. She thought for a moment, then said, "No—I was wrong. I guess he will like it. In fact, you may have a hard time getting rid of him after a while."

Joshua looked at his father. "That'd be okay, wouldn't it?"

His father, still smiling, nodded slowly.

" 'Take care! don't do your good deeds publicly, to be admired, for then you will lose the reward from your Father in heaven. When you give a gift to a beggar, don't shout about it as the hypocrites do— blowing trumpets in the synagogues and streets to call attention to their acts of charity! I tell you in all earnestness, they have received all the reward they will ever get' " (Matt. 6:1-2).

Discussion Questions:
1. Why didn't Mr. Wiggins want Denise to tell people that he and his family were helping the little boy? What do you think about people you know who brag when they do something good or charitable?
2. In what ways is Mrs. Wiggins answering Jesus' love call?
3. In what ways other than taking a bath might the little boy be cleaned up? See if you can find the scripture verses Mr. Wiggins was referring to when he said that cleaned pigs go back to wallow in their mud.

Day 3

Dark Power

Saturday morning, while Mr. Wiggins was making several phone calls, Mrs. Wiggins and Joshua sat on the couch with the little boy between them. Joshua's attention was focused on his father's phone conversations, but his mother had an arm around their guest and was speaking to him.

"Won't you please tell me your name?" she asked, as she had several times before.

The boy slowly looked up at her and studied her face. Very softly he said, "You won't use it against me?"

Mrs. Wiggins seemed surprised. "How would I use your name against you?"

"The dark power. . . ." the boy mumbled, lowering his head.

"What about the dark power?"

"If I tell you my name, you can call the dark power to take me back," the boy explained with a rush of soft, frightened words.

"Take you back?" Mrs. Wiggins asked with growing concern.

"To them."

"To whom?"

"To *them*," the boy repeated impatiently. "To my mother and *him*."

"Honey, no dark power can come into *this* house," Mrs. Wiggins assured him. "It's protected against all the dark powers by a power much stronger than they are."

The boy studied her face curiously. "Stronger? But my mother has some of my hair and some of my fingernails. She can bring me back with them—if she wants to. She and her friends, that is."

"Who are her friends?" Mrs. Wiggins asked, feeling a deep discomfort. At the same time, she felt powerfully drawn to the boy, from whom she seemed to hear a weak voice calling for help.

"The witches," the boy said.

Joshua looked at him with the beginning of a grin, but his mother

95

kept him silent with a frowning glance. She asked, "Your mother calls herself a witch?"

"She *is* a witch. She tried to kill my real father. He was working on an oil derrick, and she made a pipe fall on him. His back was broken, and he almost died." He shrugged slightly. "But she said she only meant to get even with him, not kill him."

"Oh, Lord," Mrs. Wiggins murmured.

The boy instantly looked at her.

"My mother says that, too. She says, 'Oh, Lord of Darkness—'"

"Stop!" Mrs. Wiggins said at once.

Mr. Wiggins came from the kitchen, where he had been using the telephone. When his wife and the boys looked at him, he said, "The welfare office is closed today, and no one at the police department seems to know what we should do. They don't have a missing persons report, so apparently his parents aren't searching for him."

The boy pressed close to Mrs. Wiggins. "They'll call me back, and *he'll* come and get me," the boy muttered helplessly. "My stepfather hits us a lot. That's why I was stealing—to get money so my brother and sister and I could run away for good." He struggled to the edge of the couch and looked pleadingly at Mr. Wiggins. "You see, I can fight—sometimes—but Jamie and Patty Lynn are too small to fight." He sank back against Mrs. Wiggins. "But now that you've caught me, my mother and her friends will kill something and use the blood to—to see me, and then they'll get *him* to bring me back." He looked at Mrs. Wiggins. "Please, won't you let me go? If I just keep running, maybe—just maybe. . . ."

"Once you were under God's curse, doomed forever for your sins. You went along with the crowd and were just like all the others, full of sin, obeying Satan, the mighty prince of the power of the air, who is at work right now in the hearts of those who are against the Lord" (Eph. 2:1-2).

Discussion Questions:
1. In last week's chapters, Frank thought the little boy thief was the enemy, his enemy. Now, who is the enemy? By whose power do people who are "against the Lord" become rich, powerful, even famous? What are some of the results when people use that source of power? Is the little boy's problem one of the results?
2. Compare the homes of those who are *with* the Lord with what you can guess about the homes of those who are *against* the Lord. After death, what kind of "home" will each person have?

Day 4

The Choice

Mr. and Mrs. Wiggins went into their bedroom to pray, discuss the situation, and decide what they should do. Joshua, meanwhile, watched the little boy scrunch lower and lower into the couch.

"Are you trying to hide?" Josh asked him.

The boy nodded slightly, folding his arms tightly over his thin chest.

"You don't have to."

The boy looked sideways at him.

"Like my mother said, the power in this house is much stronger than the dark power you're afraid of. Do you know about God?"

The boy flinched. "Yeah," he said hesitantly. "He does bad things to people. He hurts them."

Josh overcame his surprise as he realized that in the boy's mind, the spiritual things were turned upside down. What Joshua knew to be good, the boy thought was bad; and what the boy thought was good, Joshua knew to be bad. Josh turned so the boy could see him more clearly. "Do *we* seem bad? Do you think we're going to hurt you?"

The boy shook his head.

"But we not only believe in God, we love and obey His Son, Jesus—so are we bad also?"

The boy's eyelids flickered slightly. "Jesus?"

"Yes. Jesus Christ was a part of God, but He came down from heaven and became a baby boy. He grew up, never did anything wrong, and died of His own free will, as a sacrifice, so God wouldn't have to punish anyone who believes in Jesus."

"Sacrifice?" the boy asked, sitting upright. "My mother and her friends raise goats so they can sacrifice them to—"

"No," Joshua interrupted. "That's the opposite of what Jesus did. Do your mother and her friends kill things so they can make the dark power happy?"

97

The boy nodded.

"Well, Jesus died for the opposite reason: for *our* happiness, so that we could be God's children. If He hadn't died to pay for all the bad things we've done, you and I would have to face God all dirty and bad—and God's goodness can't stand that. We'd be punished in hell, unless we let Jesus be our Lord instead of the other power—the power you're so afraid of." He watched for the boy's reaction, but he seemed lost in thought. Gently, Josh said, "You're afraid, aren't you—of the dark power, your mother, your stepfather? Aren't you tired of hurting and being hurt, of stealing and getting caught, of running and of seeing your brother and sister hurt?"

Tears formed in the boy's eyes as he searched Joshua's face. "I—I've never heard *any* of this before," the boy said in a rush of words. "Who—who are you, and how do you know these things?"

"My name is Joshua—Joshua Wiggins, and I know these things from the words God told us—in the Bible, His book. I also know them because of what I've seen and done and what I've seen happen to other people." He gave the boy a moment to think. "Do you want to be like me and my parents, and worship the Lord of *Light*—or do you want to be like your mother, her friends, and your stepfather, and worship the lord of darkness?"

The boy trembled and shrank back; Josh leaned toward him and placed both hands on the boy's shoulders.

"Please, don't be afraid," Josh said quietly. "Let Jesus take your badness and your fear—and your pain."

The boy continued to tremble, caught in the middle of a battle in which two powers were pulling on him from each side. At last, he collapsed onto the couch. Joshua barely heard him whisper, "I—don't want to be bad. I want to be good." He turned his head toward Joshua. "But Joshua, I'm *scared!*"

"Come to me and I will give you rest—all of you who work so hard beneath a heavy yoke. Wear my yoke—for it fits perfectly—and let me teach you; for I am gentle and humble, and you shall find rest for your souls; for I give you only light burdens" (Matt. 11:28-30).

Discussion Questions:
1. Describe what you think our lives would be like if Jesus had not come to us.
2. Why is "peace with God" so important? Why, for example, did the angels announce Jesus' birth by saying, " '. . . and peace on earth for all those pleasing him' " (Luke 2:14b)? And why did Jesus,

98

after rising from death, greet His disciples with, " 'Peace be with you' " (John 20:19b, RSV)? In what way(s) is the little boy lacking that peace?

3. Would you be willing to offer yourself as evidence of what Jesus can do, as Joshua did? If you were Joshua, what else would you do or say to the little boy?

Day 5

Protection

Monday, after school was over, Joshua, Chris, and the other King's Kids hurried to the Wiggins' house. They all were curious as to what Mr. and Mrs. Wiggins had found out about the little boy. Joshua led the group inside, but they could find no one. Joshua hurried through the house, calling for his parents, then went into the garage. There, he found his father—building a bed with the help of the little boy, who was now grinning.

Mr. Wiggins laid down his hammer as Mrs. Wiggins stood from a chair at one side and went to lay one hand on the boy's back.

Mr. Wiggins looked at the King's Kids. "Well, did you all come by to raid our refrigerator?"

"No, Dad," Joshua said. "Stop teasing and tell us. Who is he?"

"And can he stay here?" Chris inquired.

"And—" Denise began, but stopped when Mr. Wiggins laughed and raised one hand.

He put one hand on the boy's back beside his wife's hand and knelt beside him. "Do you want to tell them your name?"

"Mark," the boy said, pulling a splinter from the side of the bed frame. He glanced at Joshua. "Mark Miller." He blushed and looked up at Mr. Wiggins.

Mr. Wiggins stood and said firmly, "Will none of you gossip?" When each of the King's Kids had nodded, he continued, "The welfare supervisor and I have had two long talks today, one down at his office, one here. It seems that the police have arrested Mark's stepfather—for child abuse. His mother, Grace, has apparently left town; at least, the police haven't been able to find her. We have applied for temporary custody of Mark—and of his brother and sister if they can be found. So, Mark has a home, at least for a while—probably a long while."

The King's Kids gathered closely around Mark and Mr. and Mrs.

100

Wiggins. Denise stuck out her right hand and awkwardly said, "Welcome to the club!"

"Yeah," Chris added, beaming. "And say, do you need some clothes? We've got some clothes Randy hardly wore before he outgrew them."

"And my parents have a mattress that looks about right for this bed," Janie Warren said, rubbing one hand along Mark's headboard.

They each added something, and the gathering took on a party mood—until Mark's smile disappeared and he turned away and tried to leave the group.

Mrs. Wiggins knelt and took him in her arms. Looking over his shoulder, she told the King's Kids, "We appreciate your help, but don't forget: More than anything else we can do, we *must* pray. This battle isn't over, by any means."

"Yeah," Seth Jensen said in a sad tone, "the other side still has prisoners, doesn't it?"

Just then, someone cleared his throat. The King's Kids turned —and saw that Frank Rothman had come into the garage, looking embarrassed and out of place. He evidently had followed the group to the Wiggins' house, and in their happiness they had neither heard nor seen him standing by the door—although Mark had. Frank cautiously went through the group to Mark and knelt by him. "I—I feel real bad about what I did," he said. "My stepfather doesn't treat me exactly like a prince, either, so I wish I'd taken time to listen to you, to learn about you—before I tried to beat you up." Blushing, he tried to turn so none of the others could see him as he added, almost in a whisper, "Will you forgive me?"

Mark looked at him with sudden confusion. "Forgive you?"

Frank nodded. "Yeah, for not letting you see Jesus in me. I failed again."

Denise went at once to Frank, knelt by his side, and grasped his hand. But he looked only at the boy.

"I—forgive you," Mark muttered, then boldly looked at Frank. "But I *do* see Jesus in you." He stood and turned to look at the King's Kids, "Whatever it is I see in all of you—if that's Jesus, then I want to be His, too. Can I?"

"I pray that you will begin to understand how incredibly great his power is to help those who believe him. It is that same mighty power that raised Christ from the dead and seated him in the place of honor at God's right hand in heaven, far far above any other king or ruler or dictator or leader. Yes, his honor is far more glorious than that of

101

anyone else either in this world or in the world to come" (Eph. 1:19-21).

Discussion Questions:
1. Who actually saved Mark? Why? How?
2. In what way did Frank fail? In what way did he succeed? Which was more important, his failure or his success?
3. Of what kind of home, other than the Wiggins' house, is Mark now a member? How can he be protected there? What are the best things Mark—and the members of his new family—now can do about his mother, brother, sister and stepfather?

WEEK EIGHT
Seeds

Day 1

Lady in Hiding

The school year drew to an end, and Mark Miller remained with the Wiggins family. His mother, brother and sister still had not been located, and his stepfather had jumped bail and apparently left the state. In the meantime, Mark had seemed—to Mrs. Wiggins at least—like a planted seed; he had sprouted, spiritually, and grown rapidly. He had learned to pray, and he had memorized several verses from the Gospel of Mark. Joshua and the King's Kids, meanwhile, had gotten him used to school and had watched him lose his fear and his pained look. Just what kind of person he really was became more clear one night at supper.

After Mr. Wiggins prayed the blessing, the family began eating—except Mark. He was frowning slightly. Joshua glanced at him and wondered if school work or another student was giving him trouble. Mark saw Josh's look and said, "Do you remember that old lady who used to go all over the place picking up cans?"

"Mrs. Wards?" Joshua asked.

Mr. Wiggins stopped his loaded fork in midair. "Mrs. Wards has been picking up cans? Why?"

"According to Seth," Josh explained, "she sells them for money to pay her bills."

Mr. Wiggins looked at his wife with concern, as Mark asked, "Is she sick? I haven't seen her around in a while."

"No, I don't think so," Josh answered. "But we've been so busy thinking about you and about the camping trip this summer that we—that I've forgotten about her. I wonder how her dog is." He slowly resumed eating.

When supper was over and the dishes had been washed, Mark went to Mrs. Wiggins. "Would it be okay if I went to see Mrs. Wards?"

"I'll go with you," Josh said, watching his mother's approving nod.

The street lights were flickering on as the two boys hurried up the sidewalk. When they arrived, Mrs. Wards' house was dark. Josh knew she never went out—she had no car and very few friends—so he knocked on her front door—loudly, for he knew how hard of hearing she was. He knocked a number of times, waiting several minutes between each set of knocks. Once, Mark touched his arm and pointed to the curtained front windows, but when Josh looked, no one was there. Nor did anyone come to the door.

"Let's check around back," Josh suggested, jumping off the porch. Almost immediately, from the kitchen area, Mrs. Wards' fox terrier began barking.

Josh said, "I don't like this. It's like she's in hiding." He went to the back door and loudly called, "Mrs. Wards! It's Joshua Wiggins—Dan Wiggins' grandson! Will you come to the door, please?" When the dog stopped barking but no one came, Josh tried to open the screen door. It was securely hooked. They waited a few more minutes, but no sounds or lights came from the house.

Joshua sighed. "Well, we might as well go home," he suggested. "We can come back tomorrow after school."

"And what if she still doesn't answer?"

"We'll call the paramedics and police and get them to break in. We can't leave her in there if something's wrong with her."

Worrying about the possibility that Mrs. Wards had run out of food or had fallen or was sick, Josh thoughtfully led Mark home.

"All of you together are the one body of Christ and each one of you is a separate and necessary part of it" (1 Cor. 12:27b).

"If one part suffers, all parts suffer with it, and if one part is honored, all the parts are glad" (1 Cor. 12:26).

Discussion Questions:
1. What does Mark's concern for Mrs. Wards tell you about him?
2. Why didn't Joshua just say he'd go to Mrs. Wards' house the next day or just try to call her or find out about her from someone else?
3. In what way(s) can a group of human beings be "the one body of Christ"?

Day 2

Persistence

"Well?" Mark asked, brushing brown hair away from his gray eyes. He was sitting on his bed.

Joshua, at his desk, glanced at Mark. "Mother needs to cut your hair again," he said, continuing to do his homework.

"Are we going or not?"

"Your hair sure grows fast," Josh said, flashing him a grin.

Mark sighed and slumped on his bed, folding his hands in his lap. He waited silently until Joshua had finished answering his science questions. Josh stood, and Mark practically ran out the door.

When Josh caught up with him on the street, he asked, "How come you're so concerned for Mrs. Wards? You didn't know her, did you?"

Mark held his head back slightly as he thought. Finally he said, "She's sort of like me, you know? Or like I *was*."

"Um," Josh allowed, and broke into a run. Mark shot past him and beat him by two yards to Mrs. Wards' front door. They knocked in unison.

They knocked and knocked, and finally they heard a faint voice from inside. "Go away," the woman's voice crackled. "Just go away!"

"No, ma'am!" Joshua said firmly. "If you don't let us see that you're all right, we're going to call the paramedics and the police!"

After a few seconds, they heard the metallic sounds of a lock, a bolt, and a chain being released. Slowly the front door opened.

Mrs. Wards' face appeared behind the screen door; her cheeks were sunken and pale. Joshua tried his best not to sound distressed as he said, "What's wrong? Are you sick?"

Mrs. Wards shook her wrinkled face, making wisps of unbrushed gray hair move slightly atop her head. "Nothing's wrong," she said, leaning against the door frame.

Mark stepped forward so she could see him. "Remember me? We

used to watch each other picking up cans."

She squinted at him, coming slightly more into the light from the outdoors. "Oh—yes, you're that little urchin—but you were dirty and your clothes didn't fit right. What's happened to you?"

Mark grinned at Joshua. "The Wigginses took me in. I'm living with them now." He frowned. "But what about you? How come you haven't been out? It's been more than a month since I've seen you."

Mrs. Wards' fox terrier appeared in the doorway; he stood with his front paws against the screen and whined. Even he looked thin and sad. Mrs. Wards said, "I suppose I'm just not one to burden other people with my problems. This house—all my bills. . . ." Her face took on such a pained look that Mark pressed his hands on the screen and made a funny sound. Joshua looked at him; the boy was crying. Mrs. Wards bent down to look at his face.

"Why are you crying?" she asked.

"Be—because you're all alone here," Mark said, "and you won't let anyone help you."

"Oh, no one wants to be bothered with an old woman," she said with a shrug. Mark still was crying. "Please, don't cry," she said, making an effort to brighten. "Please, honey, I'm not worth *that*."

"You *are*!" Mark said almost angrily. "If I am, *you* are!"

Mrs. Wards opened the screen door, and Mark immediately entered so he could hug up against her. She held her arms away from him, then slowly curled them around his back. Her twisted, spotted hands began to stroke Mark's hair. "Please, honey," she said, "don't cry."

"When Jesus saw [Mary, the sister of Lazarus] weeping and the Jewish leaders wailing with her, he was moved with indignation and deeply troubled. 'Where is he buried?' he asked them. They told him, 'Come and see.' Tears came to Jesus' eyes" (John 11:33-35).

Discussion Questions:
1. Why was Mark crying? Why did Jesus cry? Read Romans 12:15; What does that verse tell us about Jesus' love call?
2. What would you do next if you were Joshua?

Day 3

The Collection

Joshua and Mark talked with Mrs. Wards for a short while, then went straight home. Mark silently watched Josh calling the King's Kids. Within an hour, Chris, Lori, Janie, Sammy, Richard, Seth, Denise, Frank and David were gathered with them in the Wiggins' den.

Joshua explained the situation and ended by saying, "We could do several things. For example, we could pool part of our money—even the money we've been saving for the camping trip—and give it to Mrs. Wards to help her pay her bills and buy food. We could also work and give part or all of our earnings to her."

"Work?" Sammy asked, making a face as if someone had just asked him to take a bath.

"Sure," Josh began. "We can mow yards, pick up aluminum cans—"

Frank interrupted, "*I'm* not picking up any more cans!"

"Why not?" Mark asked. The other kids turned and looked at him as if he had just appeared. He blushed and hunched his shoulders.

" 'Cause it's *embarrassing,*" Frank said. Most of the kids were looking at him with critical frowns. "Look, *you* may like walking in dusty ditches an' having people drive by an' stare at you, but I don't like it. I'd rather clean swimming pools or—or—"

"If there's a whole bunch of us," Denise said, leaning toward him, "then you won't be by yourself and won't feel like they're staring at you." She smiled at Joshua. "Got some sacks?"

"We oughta split up," Richard suggested. "There won't be enough cans in one place for all of us to pick up—unless a convention of drunks stopped somewhere."

"They did," Janie said, wrinkling her nose. "Out at North Lakes Park there's a place where Pa-pa and I like to fish. There're cans all over the place—around the picnic tables, in trash cans—"

"You're going to dig in trash cans?" Frank demanded. "Like the bums do?"

"You don't have to go, you know," Chris said bluntly.

Frank glared at him. Slowly, his hard look wilted and he shrugged. Finally, he grinned. "No, I'll go—and I'll bet I can pick up more'n the rest of you. At least I've had practice at it."

"*We*'ve had practice, too," Mark said with a grin.

"Of course, I don't mean that those who receive your gifts should have an easy time of it at your expense, but you should divide with them. Right now you have plenty and can help them; then at some other time they can share with you when you need it. In this way each will have as much as he needs" (2 Cor. 8:13-14).

Discussion Questions:
1. What do the King's Kids have to share other than money? What might Mrs. Wards share with them in return?
2. What is Frank's problem, his real objection, in this chapter?
3. Why don't the King's Kids simply wait for their parents, or some social welfare agency, or their church to do something for Mrs. Wards?

Day 4

Sharing

Four days' dirty, sweaty, smelly work netted the King's Kids enough sacks of flattened cans to fill the back of the Warrens' van. Pa-pa Warren volunteered to drive the kids and their cans to the recycling center Saturday afternoon.

At the center, the kids formed a chain to pass the sacks to Pa-pa so he could dump them into a bin. The attendant weighed them, then took Pa-pa to an office and paid him, while a machine shot the cans into a truck trailer. Pa-pa soon came from the office, counting a small stack of bills and grinning. The kids piled into the van, and he climbed behind the steering wheel with a satisfied grunt. "Better'n sixty dollars," he announced.

"All right!" Richard exclaimed.

"That's pretty good," Joshua said, smiling back at Pa-pa.

"Aw, that's less than my grandmother sends me at Christmas," Frank said tiredly, flopping against his seat.

Pa-pa turned and levelled a stern gaze at him. "It's seeds," he said. When the kids looked curiously at him, he added, "Remember when Jesus asked His disciples to search for food among the crowd that was hungry? All they could come up with were some loaves of bread and a few fishes. Why do you suppose Jesus bothered to ask? Why didn't He just make food appear?"

When no one else answered, Mark hesitantly said, "I guess He had to start somewhere."

Pa-pa flashed Mark a huge smile and nodded. "Jesus wants us to offer up whatever we have—even a tiny bit of faith—or sixty-three dollars and forty-two cents—and let Him work with it." He nodded again to Mark. "You wait an' see!" He started the van and drove to Mrs. Wards' house.

With the kids fanned out behind him, Pa-pa Warren knocked loudly on Mrs. Wards' door. When she opened it—and promptly put her hands to her shrunken cheeks in astonishment—he presented her with the money. "And if you want me to go pay your bills, I will," he said firmly.

"Oh, thank you, Lon," Mrs. Wards said. Tears brimmed her reddened lids as she looked beyond him at the King's Kids. "And thank you! Did you have to work very hard for this?"

"Naw," Frank replied offhandedly, "not so hard. It was fun, actually." He grinned at his friends, but few of them returned the grin.

"It's not from your allowances, is it?" Mrs. Wards asked with sudden concern, holding the money toward them in her trembling hands.

"No, ma'am," Joshua said. "We picked up cans—like you used to."

She sighed and smiled. "That was nice, actually. I learned a lot from collecting cans—humility, for one thing, and meekness, for another. Besides, I got good exercise." She drew herself upright and smiled again. "In fact, now that the burden of worrying about paying the worst of my overdue bills is off my mind, I think I'll start getting out again—if you kids haven't picked up all the cans!"

The King's Kids laughed, and Chris said, "If we have, all you'll have to do is wait for another weekend and the ditches will be full."

"But this isn't all," Joshua said quickly, nodding toward the money. "We're not going to let you go into hiding again." He hesitated. "Will you tell us how much money you need each month?"

"Oh, honey, you couldn't raise that much—not even if you picked up all the cans in the county." Joshua and the others stared at her resolutely. She sighed. "I need almost four hundred dollars more than my Social Security check pays." The kids looked at one another; she saw that some of the wind had been taken out of their sails.

Pa-pa turned to the kids, and in a strong voice he said, "Remember what I told you? Seeds!"

" 'The meek and lowly are fortunate! for the whole wide world belongs to them' " (Matt. 5:5).

Discussion Questions:
1. What benefits—or blessings—did Mrs. Wards see in picking up aluminum cans? What blessings do you think the King's Kids received?
2. Are we supposed to take Jesus' "Sermon on the Mount" seriously? Did He really mean that meek and lowly people own the world? Look up the words "meek" and "lowly" and see if you can tell what Jesus meant. Matthew 11:29-30 may help you, for in those verses Jesus says that He himself was (and is) what He urged us to be.

Day 5

The Seeds Take Root

The last Sunday before the end of school, Pastor Burton asked Joshua to call a meeting of the King's Kids. The next afternoon, all of them were gathered in Joshua's den, wondering what Mr. Burton wanted. When he arrived, he was greeted with a barrage of questions.

He held up both hands as if in surrender and sat where they all could see him. He sighed through a broad smile. When they were quiet, he said, "Some people have nothing better to do with their time than talk about crime, inflation, and other problems. *But*," he said more loudly to quench their budding questions, "but a few other people—such as one oil-well equipment salesman in particular—spend much of their time listening for *good* news. And this man heard a bit of good news last week that made him instantly reach for his checkbook. He heard that about a dozen kids had spent four days picking up cans to help a lonely old lady pay her bills." He paused, and several voices erupted instantly with questions.

"What'd he do?"

"Did he pay the rest of her bills?"

"Who is he? What's his name?"

Pastor Burton raised his hands in surrender again. "He doesn't want his name known, and what he did can't even come off his income tax. He set up a trust fund for Mrs. Wards that will pay her a minimum of four hundred dollars a month for the rest of her life. And when she dies—"

"Dies!" Mark said, sitting forward on his chair.

"And when she dies, the money will go to someone else—someone you kids choose. A Mr. Saling at the First State Bank will be the one you get in touch with." The pastor leaned back in his chair as the kids looked at one another with quiet joy.

"Now we can relax," Frank said, clasping his hands behind his head.

113

Joshua gave him a peculiar look but said nothing.

"So," Janie Warren said quietly, looking at Chris and Josh, "it was like Pa-pa told us—our seeds sprouted."

"And grew!" Mark said, and dashed out the door to visit Mrs. Wards.

"But remember this—if you give little, you will get little. A farmer who plants just a few seeds will get only a small crop, but if he plants much, he will reap much. Every one must make up his own mind as to how much he should give. Don't force anyone to give more than he really wants to, for cheerful givers are the ones God prizes. God is able to make it up to you by giving you everything you need and more, so that there will not only be enough for your own needs, but plenty left over to give joyfully to others" (2 Cor. 9:6-8).

Discussion Questions:
1. Who were the cheerful givers in this story? What does Paul, in the Scripture quoted above, say God promises them?
2. Why didn't Mrs. Wards' benefactor want his name known?
3. Why did Joshua give Frank a "peculiar look" after Frank said, "Now we can relax"?

WEEK NINE

Emory Peak

Day 1

The Long Drive

School was out and grades were in; the great freedom of summer vacation had begun again! All the King's Kids had passed to the next grade, and nine eager, impatient boys were sitting in either the Wiggins' station wagon or the Warrens' van. The back of each vehicle was crammed with ice chests, sleeping bags, tents, backpacks, boxes of groceries. Mr. Warren, David's father, and Mr. Wiggins were studying the map one final time, while David, Chris, Joshua, Frank, Seth, Richard, Sammy, Randy Dobbs and Mark Miller sat waiting, listening with unconcealed anxiousness to begin.

Mr. Wiggins was tracing highway lines with one forefinger. "It's a long drive to Big Bend National Park," he said as if warning the boys.

"And when we get there," Mr. Warren added, "there'll be desert camping and the long climb up Emory Peak—all 7,835 feet of it." He looked at the younger boys to see if their determination was holding firm.

"Let's go!" Randy said, rocking on the front seat of the station wagon. "I'm tired of sitting here."

Mr. Wiggins looked solemnly at Mr. Warren and told Randy, "If you're tired of sitting now, how'll you feel after riding ten hours?"

"How'll *you* feel after driving that long?" Joshua asked, rubbing his father's back where he knew his father got tense from driving.

Mr. Wiggins laughed as he folded the map and threw it onto the dashboard. "Let's pray for strength *and* a safe trip," he said, taking his son's hand in one of his large hands.

117

Once the tiny caravan was on the highway, the boys spent the first hour staring ahead out the windows. Then they began to get bored. They began counting out-of-state license plates and competing to see how many different states they could spot. When that got old, they tried counting horses, with bonus points for white ones. Next, they tried counting cars in a freight train they passed. All the while they fidgeted, slumped, leaned, and tried to ease their cramped muscles. Finally, Mr. Wiggins headed into a roadside park so they could eat lunch; Mr. Warren parked behind him.

A scramble began—to the restroom, into the grocery boxes and ice chests, to the drinking fountain. Almost immediately, the boys discovered that fixing lunch out of boxes and ice chests isn't quite the same as having a mother set it on a table; the wind blew potato chips and napkins away—and it blew dust into sandwiches and drinks. Soon, though, they were on the road again, although it seemed they were going very slowly at fifty-five when cars went whizzing past them.

The sun crawled toward the west, making the inside of the vehicles hot despite air conditioning. The boys' clothes stuck to them; their cramped spaces seemed even smaller than they had seemed that morning.

"How much longer?" Seth asked Mr. Wiggins, whining slightly.

"A long way," Mr. Wiggins said, flexing his shoulder muscles to loosen them. "Almost all day tomorrow, too."

"I wish my father could have flown us there," Chris said sourly.

"How would you have liked crossing the prairies and deserts in a horse-drawn wagon?" Joshua asked, leaning against the dashboard to give Chris more room to stretch for a while. Chris groaned as he stretched.

The grumbling continued until finally Mr. Wiggins laughed, then said, "Think about this: 'And let us not get tired of doing what is right, for after a while we will reap a harvest of blessing if we don't get discouraged and give up.'"*

"Let's count telephone poles," Mark said.

"Aw, that's boring," Chris replied, slumping and closing his eyes. Before long, all the boys except Joshua had found some folded up, cramped position fit for sleeping. The station wagon became silent except for the humming of tires against pavement.

"[Jesus told them,] '. . . and many of you shall fall back into sin and betray and hate each other. And many false prophets will appear

---

*Galatians 6:9

118

and lead many astray. Sin will be rampant everywhere and will cool the love of many. But those enduring to the end shall be saved' " (Matt. 24:10-13).

Discussion Questions:
1. In what way could the boys' trip be compared with the Christian life?
2. In what way has Mr. Wiggins set a Christian example?

Day 2

Wings Like Eagles

Since none of the boys had been camping in a year or so—and some, such as Frank Rothman, had never been camping—their first night in a sleeping bag on hard ground was strange and uncomfortable. Frank kept waking up—then sitting upright, staring at the star-sprinkled sky and the dark, swaying tree branches overhead in the campground. He slept very little, as did several others. Thus, the next day's travel was sprinkled with small fights and arguments. And the miles went past with great monotony.

"You did, too!" Frank said. "You *deliberately* stepped on my foot!"

"I did not!" Sammy protested. "You've got me jammed against this door so I can't even move."

Mr. Warren pulled into the next filling station. As he got out, he leaned into the backseat and very quietly said to Frank, "Would you like something to cool you off?" He glanced at the other boys and led the way to the refreshment center.

When they reached the junction at Marathon, the boys cheered as they read the sign: "Big Bend National Park—69 miles." Soon they were approaching the park entrance. Mr. Wiggins told his passengers, "The park is 1,100 square miles, and most of it is the northern part of the Chihuahuan Desert. A number of mountain ranges are near the park, and all of one range—the Chisos, or Ghost, Mountains—is in it. The Rio Grande River, which divides Mexico from the United States, makes the 'big bend' of the park; the river runs through several deep canyons—but we won't take a rafting trip through them this time."

The boys stared out the windows, pointing to the infrequent ranch houses and to the many strange desert plants.

Late that afternoon, Joshua suddenly leaned forward as a creature raced across the road. "A pig!" he said, grinning that he had seen their first wild animal.

120

"A javelina," Mr. Wiggins said, slowing the station wagon so the boys could watch the animal race down an arroyo.

After going a few more miles, Chris nudged Josh and pointed to a low-slung, brown, white and black animal waddling along the roadside. "Badger," Chris said, looking at Mr. Wiggins. "Isn't it?"

Mr. Wiggins nodded. "Not like a zoo, is it?"

"Are there other wild animals here?" Randy asked in a small voice.

"Cougars, some bear, coyotes, jackrabbits, skunks," Mr. Wiggins said.

"Cougars?" Randy repeated, glancing at Seth.

They stopped at Panther Junction and registered for a campsite, then made their way to the entrance of the dirt road to Glenn Springs. A sign warned, "Rough road ahead. Beware of flash floods."

"Floods?" Seth asked, gripping the front seat as the station wagon lurched and bounced down the road. "But it looks so *dry*. Hardly anything looks green—except down there along that dry creekbed."

"A desert shower would fill that to overflowing," Mr. Wiggins said, fighting the steering wheel as he guided the car around large rocks in the road. "Those showers tend to be sudden and violent."

In the van, jouncing along in the trail of billowing dust from the station wagon, Frank suddenly leaned across Richard. "Hey—hey!" he yelled. "Lookit that—that dog!"

The boys turned quickly, in time to see a gray form disappearing among long-armed, thorny plants. "That was a coyote," Mr. Warren said.

"Will it bite?" Frank asked, frowning as he clung to the seat.

"Rabbits and mice," Mr. Warren said, laughing.

The bouncing grew worse as the vehicles wound down to arroyos, crunched across gravel, then wove their way up another ridge. To their right, the boys could see mountains, which seemed to grow higher as they drove nearer. "Those are the Chisos Mountains," Mr. Warren said. "And the tallest of them is Emory Peak. They look close, but they're not."

The sun was setting as the two vehicles lurched down the side of a ridge and into the broad canyon formed by a creek. "Water!" the boys cried, seeing cattails and willows and the glint of sunlight on the surface. They had been staring at seemingly barren, parched desert for so many hours that the sight of water seemed heavenly. "Can we go swimming?" Frank asked.

"First, we've got to set up camp and cook supper," Mr. Warren said. "Then you may swim or go exploring."

121

When the van and the wagon stopped in the circular campground, the boys noticed that no one else was there. They climbed out and stretched their muscles—and then they noticed It.

Seth was standing motionless. "Sure is quiet," he whispered to Randy.

Randy listened. There were no motors, no planes, no televisions, no anything—only silence. A few crickets and other insects were droning, but their noise seemed as nothing inside the vast, empty silence of the desert. The boys found themselves swallowing hard with dry mouths and standing close together, shivering from the chill evening air. Mr. Warren went to Frank. "Want to go exploring after supper?"

"N-no!" Frank said quickly.

In silence, the boys began unloading the vehicles, often staring off into the quiet darkness. Hulking, shadowy mountains stood all around the horizon beneath an awesome sky of deep blue, filled with more stars than the boys had ever seen—stars brighter than they'd ever seen.

"I—I'm scared," Seth whispered to Randy, who said, "Me too!"

Mr. Wiggins fired up a camp stove. Standing in its light, he proclaimed:

" 'But they that wait upon the Lord shall renew their strength. They shall mount up with wings like eagles; they shall run and not be weary; they shall walk and not faint' " (Isa. 40:31).

Discussion Questions:
1. Of what, other than wild animals, were the boys frightened? In what way were they "closer" to God than they had been at home?
2. Why do you suppose Mr. Wiggins chose to quote from Isaiah? Why might the boys need to remember that verse?
3. Why is "waiting upon the Lord" important?

Day 3

Desert Crossing

In the morning, just before dawn, the boys woke and climbed out of their tents. They stood and stared about with strange looks on their faces. Josh grinned and told Chris, "Doesn't look anything like it did last night."

Chris was not grinning. "Looks pretty gruesome to me."

David came to them, his hands stuffed in his pockets. "Yeah," he muttered. "Never saw so many rocks."

"But look how far you can see," Josh said, pointing around them at the mountains in the hazy distance. He turned toward the east, where the sky was becoming yellow. Before long, the sun peeped above the mountains and shot broad lances of yellow over the desert. The sight of the sun cheered the boys, and they set about helping the men cook breakfast.

They spent the day exploring the creek and its canyon, climbing up smooth, dry waterfalls, picking up bones and looking at the seemingly endless kinds of rocks. Seth and David took Mr. Wiggins' plant identification book and went off to see how many different plants they could find. They came back about lunch time with their results.

"There are more'n fifty-six kinds of bushes and cacti out there."

"And about fifteen kinds of flowers—all blooming!"

"And six kinds of trees."

Frank sniffed smugly. "Well, we found cougar and coyote tracks by a pool, and we heard a bunch of those wild pigs snorting."

By the end of the day, they were more accustomed to the desert, and that night they slept soundly. It was good that they did.

The next day, they packed their backpacks, looking frequently toward the Chisos Mountains, which Mr. Wiggins had said were about seventeen miles away. "Can we walk that far?" Randy whispered to David, who shrugged and shouldered his pack.

Mr. Warren—who was going to drive the van up to the Basin to pick the group up after their hike—watched Mr. Wiggins lead the single file of boys up a ridge and disappear into the desert. He prayed a while for their safety, then locked up the remaining gear in the station wagon and drove slowly out of the canyon.

The boys enjoyed the first few miles of the hike. The desert air was more pure than any air the boys had breathed; the light was brighter; and there was a sense of adventure in looking for animals. Though they said little, the boys were awed by their surroundings—by the harsh-looking desert, by the majestic mountains standing faintly purple in the distance, and by the unbounded sky overhead.

"Hawks," Josh said, pointing skyward to show Chris.

Chris stumbled, holding his pack straps off his shoulders with his thumbs. "Um," he said, shaking one foot at Josh. "Blisters."

"Blisters?" Mr. Wiggins asked, stopping. He unshouldered his pack and took out a can of powder. "Change your socks and use this," he told Chris. To the other boys, he said, "And all of you, make sure you drink more water than you want. The humidity is less than three percent, so your body loses water without your even knowing it. We'll camp tonight by a spring where you can refill your canteens."

Richard, for one, thought the advice was rather pointless. He didn't feel thirsty, and he wasn't even sweating. But after going another two miles, his feet began feeling very heavy; finally he stumbled and fell. When Josh and Richard rushed to him, Josh said to his father, "He's white and clammy."

"I feel sick," Richard moaned as Chris helped him take off his pack.

David, Seth, and Mark looked at one another, and they seemed to share the same fear: *What if we get sick out here—and maybe die? Who could help us—and where could we go for help?* While Mr. Wiggins gave Richard tablets of salt and other minerals and made him drink, the younger boys looked around anxiously. They could see absolutely no sign of human life.

Soon, Richard was able to stand and slowly proceed, with Mr. Wiggins carrying Richard's pack as well as his own. But after a while, Joshua—then Chris—took Richard's pack and carried it. The group's pace became slower and slower. They kept their eyes on Emory Peak—their goal—but even though they knew the peak was getting closer, it seemed farther away, and their own strength seemed less and less adequate for making such a trek.

They ate their lunch in silence, and the afternoon rest stops did little to restore their strength. Most of the boys' canteens were almost empty, and all of their feet were sore. Their shins and ankles had been punched by sharp-pointed lechugilla leaves. Their exposed skin was turning red and wind-parched. Their lips and eyes were dusty dry, and their mouths seemed lined with cotton. As they trudged in a staggering line up the loose rock face of another, higher ridge, hope seemed to be fading like the daylight. They could feel the evening chill coming on, and with it came doubt—and fear.

"There's the spring!" Mr. Wiggins announced as he stopped the group. He pointed toward the actual base of the Chisos Mountains, at a shadowy, tree-lined canyon that meandered down from the mountain range. The boys gulped the last of their water and hurried on, summoning what was left of their strength to reach a campsite and water before night caught them on the open desert. As he forged ahead, Mr. Wiggins called, "And just think, tomorrow we'll *really* begin to climb!" The boys glanced up at the peaks—and said not a word.

"See, God has come to save me! I will trust and not be afraid, for the Lord is my strength and song; he is my salvation. Oh, the joy of drinking deeply from the Fountain of Salvation!" (Isa. 12:2-3).

Discussion Questions:
1. When Christians become exhausted and discouraged, what would Jesus want them to do? How would singing help? What song would you sing?
2. How important is water to us? How important is salvation to us? How are they alike?

125

Day 4

Climbing

While their supper cooked on alcohol stoves, the boys huddled near one another and smelled the food, eager despite their exhaustion. An owl hooted eerily—and another answered from high in the canyon. Bats squeaked overhead, and the rising moon made flitting silhouettes of the bats. A cold wind whispered and moaned down from the heights, and the boys thought about the climb they would make. Mr. Wiggins, watching them, dug in his pack and pulled out a Bible.

"You brought that?" Frank asked. "I was wishing I'd left half my stuff in the van!"

Mr. Wiggins smiled and opened the Bible as Joshua found a flashlight and held it so his father could read. He read from the Psalms of David, ending with Psalm 45:2-4: "You are the fairest of all; your words are filled with grace; God himself is blessing you forever. Arm yourself, O Mighty One, so glorious, so majestic! And in your majesty go on to victory, defending truth, humility, and justice. Go forth to awe-inspiring deeds!" He closed the Bible and put it into his pack, then began serving supper.

As he ate, Chris managed to pause long enough to tell Josh, "God *is* majestic, isn't He? I never actually realized that—until we got here."

Josh nodded, swallowing a mouthful of stew. "And that sunrise this morning was really something!"

They tried to remember such thoughts as they rose in the chill morning before dawn, ate, packed and set off up a trail. A marker said, "South Rim: 6.6 miles," and they knew that those miles would be almost straight up. So, they went slowly, deliberately. And they tried not looking upward so often that they got discouraged. Sooner than they expected, they reached a stopping place in the looping series of switchbacks of the trail. Sinking down to rest, they unshouldered their packs and looked out over the blue-hazed vastness of the desert.

"Look how far we've come!" David said, amazed. He unscrewed the cap of his canteen and drank deeply.

Joshua and Chris stood on a boulder and tried to see Glenn Springs. They could barely see a green wandering line across the barrenness. "That's a long way to come," Chris said with a grin.

Frank was lying on his back, looking up at the peaks, still far above them. "Yeah, but look at how far we have to go."

The trail leveled out for a while, and the shade of juniper and pine trees refreshed them. The traveling went easier—until the trail began to climb again, this time quite steeply. Their hearts pounding, their legs aching, their backs threatening to cramp from the strain of pack straps, they labored upward. At one point, they looked back and down at the South Rim trail. "Ha!" said Richard, pointing to a group of older people who were taking pictures. "I wonder how *they* made it up here?"

Frank looked up at Emory Peak, looming high above them. "Bet they couldn't make it where we're going."

"We haven't made it yet," Mark reminded him, passing him by.

By late afternoon, they came to a trail marker which said, "Emory Peak trail: 1.2 miles." It seemed such a short distance, but their muscles were trembling with fatigue, and even the boys who were accustomed to playing soccer and baseball were dead tired. The younger boys, such as Seth and Randy, were trailing farther and farther behind. Mr. Wiggins stopped and told Joshua, "You go on and make camp. I'll stay with the stragglers."

Josh silently nodded and led the way upward, though Frank soon tramped past him on the narrow, twisting and rocky trail. Joshua methodically followed, watching Frank stop to breathe deeply of the thin, high altitude air, then struggle ahead, apparently determined to be first to reach the top. He was.

When the others caught up with Frank, they saw that he was staring outward, his mouth slightly open. He hadn't bothered to even unshoulder his pack or pull out his canteen. He was simply staring—at a boundless vista of mountain ranges, endless miles of desert, evening-shadowed canyons and ridges. The Basin—the center of the Chisos Mountains where a lodge, cabins, and campground were—lay below them. There, they could see tiny lights of cars crawling like specks along roads that looked like threads. The sunset was bursting across the desert to the west of the Basin, and the sky was flaming with bands of reds and oranges and yellows. Silently, the boys watched the light fade from the sky and desert as the sun disappeared behind a mountain range. In awed silence they made camp.

That night, Mr. Wiggins again read to them:

"I remember the glorious miracles you did in days of long ago. I reach out for you. I thirst for you as parched land thirsts for rain. Come quickly, Lord, and answer me. . . . Let me see your kindness to me in the morning, for I am trusting you. Show me where to walk, for my prayer is sincere. . . . Help me to do your will, for you are my God. Lead me in good paths, for your Spirit is good" (Psalm 143:5-7a, 8, 10).

Discussion Questions:
1. How do you suppose the boys felt, having reached their goal? Why were they silent when they reached it?
2. What reasons might Mr. Wiggins have had for reading the Scripture verses he chose?
3. In what ways is Mr. Wiggins being a Christ-like example?

Day 5

The Descent

As the sun began to color the horizon, the hikers awoke, shivering in the cold air. They made hot chocolate and gripped the warm cups with their chilled hands. The air was still and quiet. As they watched in silence, the gray eastern sky began to burn red. The coming light thinned the redness into pale yellow, which burst in a broad band over the mountains of Mexico. Slowly, majestically, the yellow brilliance spread, banishing the shadows on the desert floor and sending them fleeing into the canyons. Gradually, the boys were warmed by the sun's strengthening light, and they quickly forgot how dark and cold the night had been.

" 'Having such great promises as these, dear friends,' " Mr. Wiggins quoted,* " 'let us turn away from everything wrong, whether of body or spirit and purify ourselves, living in the wholesome fear of God, giving ourselves to him alone.' " He took a plastic basin from his pack, poured it full of water, and washed his face, neck, and hands. When he had finished, he looked at Joshua, who did as his father had done. The other boys then one by one also washed. Shivering but grinning, they watched the morning light spread radiance across the rugged desert.

They soon spread out and perched on boulders, pinnacles, and fallen ponderosa pines. Mr. Wiggins pointed out Lost Mine Peak and the vertical, bare granite faces of Casa Grande.

Joshua sat on a rain-smoothed rock, high on the pinnacle that formed the highest point of the mountain. Cautiously, with his hands sweating, Seth climbed to within a few feet of him. In a few minutes, Mark did the same. They listened to the singing of the wind and watched hawks soaring far, far below, scanning the slopes for game.

When Seth had nestled against the cold rock long enough to feel

---
*2 Corinthians 7:1

129

fairly safe, he glanced up at Joshua. "I sure am glad we came," he said.

"I'm glad we made it up here!" Mark said, laughing nervously. "But I'll be glad to go back down. It's funny, but I already miss being home."

"I wonder what the people back home are doing?" Seth quietly asked.

"Same things as always, probably," Mark said.

Seth was silent for a while, then brightened. "You know, this is sort of like being in church—even better maybe. I feel like God is all around us."

Joshua looked down at him and smiled. "I was thinking the same thing," he said quietly. "I was also thinking how easy it is to worship—I mean, really worship—God out here. It's as if nothing gets in the way."

"Yeah," Mark said thoughtfully, daring to look the hundreds of feet downward to pine trees pointing tiny tops at him from a slope. "It's easy to believe up here, but at home. . . ." He looked up at Josh. "That's wrong, isn't it? I mean, to not feel the same about Him every-where." Josh nodded with a look that was almost sad.

"Let's not change," Seth said. When the other two boys looked at him, he hastily added, "I mean, if we could climb this mountain—"

"Yeah," Mark said, grinning. He looked up at Joshua. "We're special, aren't we?"

Reluctantly, after lunch, the boys and Mr. Wiggins began the hike downward into the Basin. And when they passed tired hikers laboring upward, one or another of them cheerfully would say, "Keep going! It's not far now."

"In everything you do, stay away from complaining and arguing, so that no one can speak a word of blame against you. You are to live clean, innocent lives as children of God in a dark world full of people who are crooked and stubborn. Shine out among them like beacon lights, holding out to them the Word of Life" (Phil. 2:14-16).

Discussion Questions:
1. What do you think each of the boys learned from the camping trip? How might the trip change their lives?
2. In what way was Mark right in saying that he and his friends were special? In what way is each of us special?
3. What does it mean to *worship* God? What in your life makes it hard to worship Him? How could those obstacles be removed?

WEEK TEN

Dedications

DAY 1

The Storm

When the campers returned home, they parted company sadly; Mr. Wiggins took all the boys home except, of course, Joshua and Mark. As they drove into their own driveway, Mark sighed, "Made it! For once, I can't wait to take a hot, long bath!"

They scrambled out of the station wagon and began unloading their equipment. As they carried the first load toward the house, they saw Mrs. Wiggins standing near the door. Her arms were folded and she looked very distressed. Mr. Wiggins, Josh and Mark hurried to her.

"What's happened?" Mr. Wiggins asked, setting down the sleeping bags.

"Something almost unbelievable," Mrs. Wiggins said, glancing at Mark. "Mrs. Kibler had to go back to work, despite their plans, so she found what she thought was a reliable babysitter—"

"Something's happened to Elizabeth?" Josh asked, fearing the worst.

She nodded, trying to control her emotions.

Quickly, Josh, his father, and Mark stowed the camping gear in its places and followed Mrs. Wiggins into the house. They sat around the kitchen table, and Mrs. Wiggins resumed her story. "When Mrs.Kibler went to pick up the baby, she was met at the street by the babysitter, who was hysterical. It seems a friend of hers, who recently had lost her own children, had come by to visit, for sympathy I suppose. Anyhow,

133

the friend asked to take Elizabeth for a short ride; the babysitter had an errand to run, so she let the woman take the baby. She never brought Elizabeth back."

"That's terrible!" Mr. Wiggins said. "Do the police have any idea who the friend was?"

Mrs. Wiggins clasped her hands on the table and drew a deep breath, glancing at Mark. "Yes, I'm afraid they do."

"Afraid?" Josh asked, looking at Mark and seeing that the boy had turned very pale and seemed cowering before a blow. "Who is it?"

Very quietly, Mrs. Wiggins said, "The FBI was called in after a few days, in case the kidnapper took the baby across a state line. They questioned the babysitter, and she finally told them that the woman's name is—Grace Miller." She turned and held Mark by one shoulder.

"Mother," he muttered, hanging his head. Suddenly, he shoved his chair backward and ran across the den, down the hall, and into his and Josh's room.

For a while, the Wigginses sat silently. Then they reached for one another's hands and bowed their heads.

"All who listen to my instructions and follow them are wise, like a man who builds his house on solid rock. Though the rain comes in torrents, and the floods rise and the storm winds beat against his house, it won't collapse, for it is built on rock" (Matt. 7:24-25).

Discussion Questions:
1. What "house" and what "rock" did Jesus mean? Will Mark's faith stand up in this "storm"?
2. What could or should he do?
3. What could the Wigginses do to help Mark in this situation?

Day 2

Questions

Mark, Joshua and Mr. Wiggins quickly took baths, and put all their dirty clothes in the laundry room. They had just begun telling Mrs. Wiggins about the desert hike and climbing the mountain when the doorbell rang. Mr. Wiggins went—and ushered three men in gray business suits into the den. They were holding trim hats in their hands, and they seemed polite but very serious. They looked at the boys, and their eyes settled on Mark.

The first man pulled a case from his coat pocket and showed an FBI badge and ID card to the Wigginses. He then sat on a chair near Mark. "Are you Mark Miller?"

Mark, almost sullenly, nodded.

"Son, I hate to tell you this," the agent began, "but we think your mother may have taken a baby without permission of the parents."

Mark suddenly sat upright. "If she did, she won't hurt her!"

The agent leaned back slightly, turning his hat in his hands. "Well, son, our information is that she's involved with a group of people who call themselves witches. Do you know anything about that?"

Mark slowly nodded.

"We've managed to track down several of the 'coven' members, but they deny knowledge of the baby or your mother. Do you know where she might have taken the baby—if she's the one who took it?"

Mark hesitated, looking at the floor, then shook his head.

"Do you suppose she might have gone back to her father in Oklahoma?"

Mark faintly shrugged.

The agent leaned forward a few inches. "Do you suppose she and her friends are planning to use the baby in some sort of sacrifice ceremony. . . ?"

Mark glared wide-eyed at the agent. "No!" he snapped. Slowly, he softened. "Do you know where my brother and sister are?" he asked.

The agent stared at him. "Not long after you went on your camping trip, the police searched a house a few miles north of town that belongs to one of the 'coven' members. Your brother and sister were there, and they were taken into custody. Soon after that, the Kibler baby was kidnapped."

"She's getting even," Mark muttered, hanging his head again. Slowly, he raised it. "Where are Jamie and Patty Lynn? May I see them?"

"You'll have to call the welfare department," the agent said, standing. He settled his hat on his neatly cut hair. "Well, if you learn anything about your mother's whereabouts, you can spare everyone a lot of anxiety if you'll call us." He took a card from a coat pocket and handed it to Mr. Wiggins. "My number is on the card. Good day." He and the other agents turned and went out.

Mark immediately ran into his room and slammed the door.

Mrs. Wiggins nodded to Joshua's questioning look, and Josh went into the room. Mark was lying across his bed, sobbing. Josh sat by him and patted his back gently.

Mark rolled over. "It was all for nothing, wasn't it? Even now I'm not free from—from Satan!"

Josh reached to a bedside table and got his Bible. He thumbed through it, stopped, and began to read: " 'Jesus said to them, "You are truly my disciples if you live as I tell you to, and you will know the truth, and the truth will set you free." ' "* He closed the Bible and held it as he said, "The key word is 'live'—which means day by day, day after day. We can't quit; we've got to obey *His* teachings, and we can't rely on anyone else's word but His."

Mark slowly calmed down. Picking at the bedspread, he said, "I know where she might be—and I know what I've got to do."

"*We*," Josh assured him.

" 'Not all who sound religious are really godly people. They may refer to me as "Lord," but still won't get to heaven. For the decisive question is whether they obey my Father in heaven' " (Matt. 7:21).

Discussion Questions:
1. Who will judge us after death? By what standard will we be judged?
2. If Mark were one who merely sounds religious, what might he have said to Josh instead of what he did say? What should he do?
3. In what way is Joshua obeying God?

---

*John 8:31-32

Day 3

Embroidery

While Mr. Wiggins drove the boys north out of town, Mark explained, "When we first came here, we stayed in a small motel—and Mom made friends with the owner. He's the one who introduced her to my stepfather."

As they drove slowly up to the motel—two rows of tiny cabins with an office by the highway—Mark looked closely at each building. At the end of the short, dirt drive, he shook his head. "Her car's not here."

Mr. Wiggins backed up to the office. The boys followed him inside, and they rang a bell at the counter. A middle-aged man with a wild gray beard and a mane of gray hair appeared, scowling suspiciously. "Yeah?"

"Remember me?" Mark asked. The man leaned over the counter and studied the boy—then grinned.

"Oh. You're one o' hers, ain't you?"

Mark nodded cheerfully. "Is she here?"

The man scowled at Mr. Wiggins and Joshua. "She said she wasn't seein' *nobody.*"

"I'm family!" Mark protested, gripping the edge of the counter.

"Well," the man drawled, "I guess it'd be okay. She's in number 10."

Mark thanked him and ran out the door and down the drive. Mr. Wiggins and Joshua caught up with him as he was knocking on the door of the last cabin in the row behind the office. No sound came from inside.

Mark knocked again—and again, and at last he yelled, "Mother! It's me—Mark!"

Quietly, near the closed door, a woman's voice asked, "Are you alone?"

Mark hesitated, frowning, then said, "No, ma'am. I'm with friends."

The voice weakly said, "I figured this would happen, sooner or later." A lock clicked and the door opened.

The woman appeared calm and tidy. Mr. Wiggins hurried past her, barely glancing at her stringy black hair, red-lipsticked mouth, and pale face. He went to the center of the tiny room and looked down at a blanket spread on the floor. On one side of the blanket was an ashtray, a pack of cigarettes, a lighter, and a glass. And in the middle of the blanket was Elizabeth Denise Kibler. Her hair was brushed neatly, and a ribbon had been tied in a topknot curl. Her dress was immaculate. Mr. Wiggins bent down to smile at her cooing, happy face, and he saw that the hem of her dress was embroidered with the words, "Trust the Lord."

Mrs. Miller closed the door and sat nervously in a chair, looking at Mark with a frightened, very tired look. Mark said, "Mama, you—you're different. I figured—" He glanced at the glass on the blanket and saw that it was empty of liquor; he also saw that the pack of cigarettes was unopened. "I figured you'd be drunk." He grinned and turned to kneel by his mother, laying his head in her lap and hugging her. She sobbed and began to cry as she hugged him in return.

"I've been so wrong," she murmured, stroking his hair, "so terribly wrong. Can you forgive me?"

Mark nodded, keeping his head pressed against her.

She looked at Mr. Wiggins, who was watching her. "I sold my car to get money so I could live here—with her." She nodded toward Elizabeth and smiled. "When they took away the last of my kids, I couldn't think of anything but how lonely I was—and scared, too. So I took her." She smiled at the baby, and Mr. Wiggins saw the loving look in her eyes. She said, "I read the words on her dress." She looked up at Mr. Wiggins. "It was like that sweet, innocent baby with all her love was telling me. . . . Anyhow, I didn't have anything to do—except read that Bible." She nodded toward a Gideon Bible lying open on the bed. "And that's what I've been doing—reading and waiting." She wiped her eyes and stroked Mark's head again.

Mark looked up at her. "Have you asked Jesus to come into your heart and be your Lord?"

"Would He?" Mrs. Miller asked. "I—I've had another master for a long time—and the Bible says I've got to be perfect. How can *I* be *perfect*?"

Mr. Wiggins heard the despair in her tone, and he went to her. "By yourself, you can't. But what is impossible for us is possible for God. You've taken the first necessary step—you've realized that God *is* God and that you've gone away from Him because of your sins.

The next step is to turn around, turn away from sin, and change your way of living because you want to get back to God."

"I do," Mrs. Miller said, staring down at Elizabeth Denise. "More than anything, I want to be like that precious baby again."

" '... you are to be perfect, even as your Father in heaven is perfect' " (Matt. 5:48).

Discussion Questions:
1. How can we "children of wrath," who cannot even fight Satan in our own strength, ever become perfect? Read Matthew 28:18 and Ephesians 3:16-17 for help in answering.
2. Do you think it was coincidence that a Gideon Bible was in the motel room and that Mrs. Miller read it? How did the embroidery on Elizabeth's dress help her?

Day 4

Restoration

Mr. Wiggins immediately phoned the Kiblers. He and the boys then took Mrs. Miller and Elizabeth straight to the Kiblers' house. Grace Miller gave the contented baby to Mrs. Kibler, who seemed numbed by the ordeal. Denise stood close by her side and briefly examined the baby, then looked tearfully at Mrs. Miller. "Thank you!" Mrs. Kibler said. "And praise the Lord! I was beginning to think we'd never. . . ."

Denise looked at Mark and Joshua. "And thank *you*, too!" she said.

Mark grinned at Joshua and said, "We didn't do much."

Mr. Kibler placed one arm around his wife's shoulders, beamed at his baby daughter, and looked at Mark. "But you did. You're 'doers of the Word.' "* He looked at Mrs. Miller and became solemn. "You took her?"

Mrs. Miller clenched her lips and slowly nodded.

"We'll have to call the police, you know," Mr. Kibler said, his expression filled with regret.

Mark looked from Mr. Kibler to Mr. Wiggins. "Does he have to?"

Before Mr. Wiggins could answer, Mrs. Miller said, "Yes, he does." She looked at the men and slumped. Tears came into her eyes as she looked from the mother to Mr. Kibler. "Can you ever forgive me?"

"We've already done that," Mr. Kibler said, tickling Elizabeth's chin; the baby giggled.

"But Mama . . . ," Mark said, about to cry.

Mrs. Miller knelt and placed her hands on his shoulders. "You've forgiven me, they've forgiven me, and God has forgiven me. Now, if *I'm* going to be what Mr. Kibler called you—a 'doer of the Word'—then I've got to settle up with the law. Otherwise I won't ever be free."

---

*James 1:22 (RSV)

Mark went into the closing circle of her arms. "I love you, Mama."

"I love you, too—now more than ever before!"

He looked at her, swabbing his cheeks with his fist. "And now I want to obey you. I won't ever run away again."

Mr. Kibler sadly went to telephone the police.

"So get rid of all that is wrong in your life, both inside and outside, and humbly be glad for the wonderful message we have received, for it is able to save our souls as it takes hold of our hearts. And remember, it is a message to obey, not just to listen to. So don't fool yourselves" (James 1:21-22).

Discussion Questions:
1. Do you think it took courage to do what Mrs. Miller did? Why do you suppose she had that kind of courage?
2. How does Romans 8:28 apply to Mrs. Miller and Mark? To the Kiblers?

Day 5

The Love Call

Sunday morning a month later was "baby dedication day" at the church. All the babies born to members of the congregation in the past year were to be carried before the altar by their parents and dedicated to God's use. Twenty-four couples and their babies stood arrayed at the front of the church, each proudly and solemnly facing the congregation.

In the congregation were, of course, the King's Kids and their parents, along with a number of other young people from the church and their parents. Among the crowd near the back were Mrs. Miller—who had been released without charge—and Mark, Jamie and Patty Lynn. The younger children were huddled against Mark, who had told them about God and Jesus. Despite what he and his mother had told them, however, they felt very strange in the large church; they fidgeted and stared past the parents and babies toward the towering stained-glass picture of Jesus and His flock.

When the dedication ceremony concluded, the parents took their babies back to the nursery, and Pastor Burton went up to the pulpit. He preached on Samuel's dedication to God, his growing up in the temple, and his becoming a true messenger of God—a servant of the Lord. As he concluded, he moved to the center of the platform and spread his arms toward the congregation. "If any of you feels the urging of the Holy Spirit to come to the altar, to dedicate yourself to God to serve Him, do so now as we sing. . . ."

Music began, and the congregation began singing, "Wherever He Leads." Joshua and the King's Kids kept glancing at the aisles, but for the entire first verse no one came down. Joshua became aware that the words of the song were ringing in his mind—and spirit. He whispered, "Lord, I'll follow." He tensed, sensing that he was about to go down the aisle. *But why?* he wondered, feeling panicky—and resisting the feeling. *I'm already saved, and I haven't felt a need for rededication. So, why . . . ?* The pull of the song's words became stronger and stronger, and Joshua felt his resistance to their message melting like ice under a blazing sun. As his resistance melted, he felt joy pure and powerful welling up inside him. He ignored the tears running down his face as the words of the song became in him a freely-given prayer, an absolute commitment. It was then that he saw, walking forward, Mrs. Miller and Mark, with Jamie and Patty Lynn between them.

When the Miller family reached the altar near Pastor Burton, Mrs. Miller knelt with Mark; the younger ones, watching their mother and older brother, hesitantly did the same. Some people in the congregation, who knew about the kidnapping, frowned, uncertain as to what to think of her and what she'd done. Pastor Burton, however, had no uncertainty. He knelt with her. Then, for a long moment between verses of the song, there seemed to be a vast silence in the building.

Joshua felt as if he literally were being pulled from the pew and impelled down the aisle. He practically ran to the Millers. The words of the song were now his own, and joy seemed to be the light around and ahead of him. He knelt behind Mark.

Almost at once, Chris was there—then Denise. Behind her, looking awed, as he had when standing alone atop Emory Peak, came Frank Rothman. Then came Sammy and Richard, shyly glancing at each other. Lori and David Matthews came next, followed closely by Janie Warren and Janice Wiggins. Randy Dobbs suddenly burst from a pew as if he'd been hiding there, and with him came Seth Jensen. They headed straight for Pastor Burton, who now was standing facing the congregation, tears on his face. What had burst loose in the church continued, and people streamed down the aisles to join a gathering that caused some of the older members simply to shake their heads in wonder, not knowing what to think.

But Pastor Burton knew. He turned to the pianist and the music director and began singing, "Praise the Lord . . . praise the Lord . . . let the earth hear His voice. . . !"

" 'So be prepared, for you don't know what day your Lord is coming' " (Matt. 24:42).

" 'Blessings on you if I return and find you faithfully doing your work. I will put such faithful ones in charge of everything I own!' " (Matt. 24:46-47).

Discussion Questions:
1. In what ways have the King's Kids been preparing for the Lord's return?
2. What must the King's Kids do in the days to come? Read Romans 12 and list at least five things they can do.